DC SUMNER

Chronicles of Ash

Shadows Rising

Contents

Prologue

For thousands of years, a tropical island called Asmaria has thrived in isolation. No ordinary human has ever heard of or seen this island, as its inhabitants vigilantly ward off strangers. Protecting their home is their top priority. They were a peaceful people for a long time until an evil demon named Aros attacked, exploiting a large gathering of people to assail the Asmarians.

In the center of the island, the Great Tree thrived, giving life to all on the island. According to Asmarian legend, the Great Tree sprouted from the ocean, bringing the island into existence. This majestic tree was not only their single most sacred object but also an integral part of their very being. Some individuals were even bestowed with special powers by the Great Tree, enabling them to control a particular element— wind, water, fire, or earth. Determining who would become one of these 'mages' was impossible until they came of age and conjured their element for the first time.

However, for those who were not blessed, some turned to the darkness. These individuals became warriors known as the Forbidden, fighting against the Asmarians. Despite being unable to wield the elements, they possessed the uncanny ability to control shadows, siphoning bits of Aros' power.

The mages of Asmaria formed the Guild, a class of protectors for the people and resources on the island. They were led by the Guardians, mages with unmatched power in each respective element. Together, they successfully pushed back the Forbidden and defeated Aros. However, this victory was short-lived, as the Forbidden regrouped in an undisclosed location, rebuilding their forces.

Every so often, Asmaria faced attacks from small groups of the Forbidden. However, these assaults were never over-whelming, and the Asmarians consistently emerged victorious. Occasionally, they managed to capture surviving members of the Forbidden, but extracting useful information was a rare occurrence.

Among the Asmarians was a man named Augustus who rapidly developed into a formidable fire mage. From a young age, he consistently outshone his peers. Augustus married a young woman named Iris, who was skilled in the ways of water. The couple was beloved by everyone who knew them

The young couple started their family, and Iris became pregnant with a baby boy. When the boy was born, they named him Ash, hoping he would develop a fondness for flames like his father. One night, a major storm hit, with rain pouring down and lightning crackling across the sky. During the storm, the couple left the island of Asmaria with baby Ash and never returned.

The Guardians of that time discovered the missing family and dispatched a patrol to find them once the storms passed. The island was searched thoroughly, but nothing was found until one of the Asmarian beasts, the borlack—a creature resembling an enlarged wolverine with the wings of an eagle—tracked the family's scent. The borlack alerted the Guardians that the scent had left the island, prompting them to send out a scout in search of the family.

For the first time in many years, an Asmarian ventured into the realm of the non-magic people. The scent was followed all the way to New York in the United States. There, a tragic discovery awaited—the lifeless body of Iris. Beside her lay their abandoned baby, Ash, left on a park bench. The scout gently picked up the infant, offering comfort, while word was swiftly sent back to the Guardians.

By the time the scout received a reply, night had fallen. His orders were to leave the baby on the bench, tightly wrapped to trap the heat. This decision conflicted with his better judgment, but as a dedicated soldier, he followed his orders. With great care, he collected Iris's body and ascended into the sky, returning to Asmaria where she was laid to rest near the Great Tree.

The Guardians, recognizing the uncertainty of Ash's future, chose to let fate decide. They knew that as he grew older, his powers might guide him back to them

Abandoned

Lightning crackled across the night sky, casting purple flashes of luminescence throughout the darkness. Rick walked through Birkwood Park, shuddering, finding solace only in the cigarette burning between his lips. His heart raced as the cries of an infant echoed around him. Hastening his pace, he turned a bend in the concrete path, revealing a single park bench. Atop it lay a wriggling bundle—a baby boy loosely wrapped in a blanket. Thunder boomed overhead as Rick picked up the small child, cradling him in his arms and shushing him in an attempt to comfort him.

Stumbling upon an abandoned baby wasn't on Rick's agenda, and he was dumbfounded by how anyone could do such a thing. A single, middle-aged man with no wife or kids of his own, Rick had never aspired to be a father. However, fate seemed to have other plans. He flicked the cigarette's filter away, exhaling smoke into the air, and rubbed the cold from the baby's tiny fingers. Noticing a word stitched in green lettering in one corner of the blanket, he read 'Ash.'

"Ash, huh? That's an unusual name."

He contemplated what to do next as the baby looked up at him, regaining the warmth in his body. The man considered going to the police but pondered the possibility of keeping him as well. After a couple of minutes, he decided to not report this and rushed home with the child. Unsure if he was being watched, he looked over his shoulders every few meters, checking his surroundings for anyone lurking in the shadows.

His apartment wasn't far from where the baby was found, but he walked as fast as he could anyway, in fear that he would somehow be caught and get into trouble. He kicked off his shoes and made the five or so steps that it took to reach the hallway leading to the bedroom. Placing Ash onto the bed, he then grabbed his laptop off the floor and sat down next to him, researching anything baby-related. It was difficult to tell, but he figured the baby was under a year old.

Rick never pictured himself as a father; his dad was a horrible man in ways that Rick dared not speak of to anyone. He stuck to himself most of the time, never bothering to make any friends. The other guys that he worked with knew little about him and he liked it that way. It was a lonely life but one that Rick was content with.

In the days following his discovery of the baby, Rick waited and waited to hear of a missing baby. He kept thinking that perhaps this was some sort of mistake and his parents would be looking for Ash. Maybe there was a freak accident that left them separated. However, no such news came. Rick became a new father with a split decision that would change the course of his life forever.

As Ash got older, Rick began to notice a darkness within the boy. It reminded him of things he'd seen on TV where a child who seems almost normal snaps one day and becomes a monster. A lot of the time they got along fine, but there were moments where Ash would do things that scared Rick.

Once, Ash asked to go play outside to which Rick responded

by telling him no. When the boy inquired as to why he couldn't go, Rick told him that it was too dangerous and it was his job to protect him. The kid didn't care. At only six years old he got so angry that he put his little foot through a wall in the kitchen. Many events like this happened over the years but they always ended just as quickly as they started.

Any time Ash had an outburst he always showed great remorse for his actions. Rick often wondered if he was bipolar and considered taking him to a doctor, but never acted on the inclination.

Perhaps the biggest indicator that something was different about Ash occurred the night before his 13th birthday. Rick got him some clothes that he thought were pretty cool. It was a whole outfit revolving around one of their favorite superhero movies. Rick had this tradition where he'd wait for Ash to fall asleep and then bring the present out of his closet and place it next to him. This way, the gift would be there when he wakes up.

Everything was normal until the moment Rick walked back out of his room. Ash was asleep, his body twitching slightly at first. Then he began to shake more aggressively. Rick was about to try waking the boy but before he could, Ash's eyes cracked open slightly and a purple glow emanated from the eye slits. Rick approached and as he got closer the hair all over his body stood up.

The event ended and Rick slowly sat the gift down next to Ash and just watched him for a moment longer, breathing heavily. He was scared of him, but more importantly, he still loved him as his son. He knew that he would do everything in his power to protect him.

Shock and Awe

Ash didn't remember much from the night of his rescue, apart from a faint vision of a beautiful woman's face, with flashes of purple light behind it. He had no idea who she was but imagined she would be his mother because that was the most likely conclusion. This was a memory that he never told Rick about, keeping this one thing for himself.

Every day was virtually the same for them, Rick would get up and leave for work, and Ash would sit at home. He was able to get enrolled in online homeschooling and was fairly bright for someone who had interaction with only one person his entire life. In the evenings when Rick returned, they would exercise together, doing push-ups and squats, having boxing matches. Rick was very much into watching boxing, and eventually lost his beer gut, thanks to their routine sparring.

Often, the boy would ask to leave their home, but Rick declined every time. He had no idea why he wouldn't let him leave just once. Any time he'd ask, Rick would just tell him that the world was dangerous and it was his duty to protect him. That wasn't a good enough reason for Ash, he wanted something more.

Ash would look at pictures of vast landscapes, full of trees and flowers, tundras covered in snow and ice, and wonder if they were even real. He didn't know how, but Ash believed that he belonged in one of these places, away from the beige walls of this place. There were many things that he wanted to experience in his life, the feeling of sand under his bare feet as waves crash on a beach. The experience of snow falling on his face, the flakes melting on his warm skin. He yearned for friendship above all things; Rick was great to him, but sometimes it just wasn't enough.

At times, Ash would consider venturing outside the apartment on his own, but never made it out the front door for fear of repercussions. He didn't like the idea of getting into trouble. Once, he made it out onto the fire escape, where there was only enough room for one person. He crawled out onto the rickety metal, looked around, and took a deep breath. He choked on the smell of garbage and reeled back into the apartment after seeing several homeless people in the alleyway below.

Throughout his short life, Ash was aware of an emptiness inside him, a void that he couldn't fill no matter how hard he tried. He read books, watched TV, and spent hours exercising, but nothing could take away the feeling that he had some sort of darkness inside him. His anger would often get the better of him; Rick came home one night and set him off just by asking how his day was. Ash erupted, like a volcano, spewing out so much anger that it left the man shocked by the outburst.

Ash was well aware that he shouldn't be having emotional explosions like this and that Rick was doing his best. He had to remind himself that without Rick, he may very well be dead. Whenever he became angry it felt like another person had taken over his body and mind, causing him to act like a crazy person. He'd put several holes in various walls of the apartment. Rick never lashed out at him but he did make him help fix the holes.

Rick wasn't a wealthy man, and hardly had room for Ash in the apartment, which meant that his birthday presents often consisted of his favorite food or a new set of pajamas. However, this time it was a whole outfit dedicated to one of the movies they watched together quite often.

On Ash's 13th birthday, he noticed Rick was acting strange towards him. He was usually upbeat but this wasn't the case. Ash thought that maybe he just hadn't slept well. Rick was preparing some eggs and bacon while Ash slowly unwrapped his present. He knew what it would most likely be. After unraveling the paper and pulling open the box he lifted the outfit into the air.

It didn't matter that he loved the outfit that portrayed one of his favorite superheroes. It was his 13th birthday and he had reached his limit of getting clothes as presents. He steeled himself in preparation to confront his dad. He'd become resentful of the way he was forced to live. Ash was determined to get out of this apartment and see the world today.

"Hey, Dad?" he said.

"Yeah, bud, what's up?" Rick responded with his back to the boy, continuing to scramble some eggs.

Ash almost changed his mind, but doubled down and said, "I know you usually say no, but could I go out today? I mean, it is my 13th birthday after all."

Ash could see Rick visibly tense up. He laid the spatula down and turned on him. Rick's face was red, heated by anger. His fists were clenched. Ash didn't understand why he'd suddenly become so angry over this. Ash was stricken with fear at the amount of rage that welled up in Rick. He was worried the man would strike him.

Rick responded through gritted teeth, droplets of saliva flying through the air, "No! How many times do I have to tell you the same thing? When will you get it through your thick skull? It's too dangerous. You could be taken from me."

Ash was hurt and wanted to hurt Rick back. He said, "As if that'd be such a horrible thing."

With wide eyes, Rick said, "What did you just say to me?"

"Gah! I have to get out of here, you're smothering me!"

"I'm the only thing you've got! Stop being so ungrateful, why don't ya?"

"This place is a prison! I hate you!"

Quinn's Mission

Quinn bid farewell to her parents. She had been selected for her first real mission, to retrieve a boy who'd been lost to their world many years ago. The Guardians could have picked anyone she was surprised they hadn't chosen someone a bit older. When she asked why they picked her, Brandr said that they needed someone closer to the boy's age who he'd have no problem trusting.

Brandr—one of the Guardians—picked her himself. She was honored to be hand-selected for something so high priority. The boy, whose name she was told is Ash, recently developed his abilities. He told her that the boy had awakened an incredible power and she wanted to ask how he knew all this but didn't in fear of coming off as disrespectful.

She was very gifted with the ways of water, surpassing almost everyone with the same ability. Her mother asked why the Guardians didn't just go themselves to which Quinn replied, "They're too important. If the island were to be attacked while they're gone we would all be doomed."

That response didn't help as Quinn intended, but her mother let her go anyway.

The information given to her consisted of a location somewhere in America. A place called New York. She'd read about it before; it was a heavily populated area with massive buildings. They didn't know exactly what the boy looked like but knew he'd developed substantial powers. Brandr told her that she'd know him when she saw him.

She had special clothes made to help her blend in. Quinn looked herself over in a mirror and thought that she looked very silly. She ventured out, excited to go on this journey.

When she asked Brandr about the importance of this boy, he told her, "I believe that this boy will be a great warrior for Asmaria. He holds great power within him and our enemies will surely be after him. We must rescue him first and ensure he isn't brainwashed to follow the darkness."

Quinn's hair whipped through the wind as she rode atop a giant eagle. His feathers were soft and she tried taking a nap but was unable to do so thanks to her nerves. She'd never been outside of Asmaria, as most of her people, and was worried she would fail. The fear of failing on this mission gripped her tightly.

Within a few hours, they made it to land. The skyline of the city rose on the horizon. It wasn't as beautiful as her home was, but Quinn could appreciate the uniqueness of it. Tall buildings came into view and she could see the appeal of living here just from that alone. The large bird landed somewhere empty where there were no watchful eyes and dismounted, sending the bird away for the time being. She didn't know how long it would take to find Ash.

Quinn checked her pocket for the small silver whistle that would call the beast back to her and was relieved to find it. She set out towards the city, looking for identifiers that would lead to his location. Brandr had given her street names and land markers that she could use to help her.

Once she made it to the heart of the city Quinn became overwhelmed by the amount of people walking around her. *How do people live like this?* she wondered to herself. It was so cramped that she barely had enough room to walk without being pressed up against other people.

There was a rather nasty lady who yelled obscenities at her after Quinn accidentally bumped into the lady's shoulder. She saw a lot of homeless people with tents spread around all over the place. The sight saddened her deeply and she wished she could take them all with her. Asmaria had no homeless population.

After walking around for what felt like forever she finally found a small building that resembled what Brandr described to be their home. Unfortunately, two members of the Forbidden found it also. Quinn didn't have any other explanation for the two black-clad men looming in the shadows outside the building.

They hadn't noticed her yet so she climbed up onto a nearby building and watched. She needed to make sure they were enemies before she acted. She also noticed they were standing near a man lying on his back in a pile of garbage. Quinn wondered if they had killed the man. While she was pondering the situation, the front door of the apartment building burst open and a boy came flying out.

Immediately, the two men began their pursuit. Luckily for her, they weren't moving very fast, keeping a good distance from him. She leaped across the neighboring rooftops, running to get in front of Ash. When she had a comfortable distance she climbed down and walked around to a good spot where she could see him coming.

He looked up and made eye contact with her. Her stomach

clenched; she'd never felt such a connection to someone she didn't know. She found her cheeks getting warm and when he turned away she dipped back out from his sight. She hid around a corner and took deep breaths, waiting for him to come back around.

Escape

Ash didn't mean to say it, but it was too late. Rick stormed across the room, grabbing Ash by the throat. He shoved him hard into the coffee table, spilling its contents onto the floor. Ash tried to retaliate with a one-two combo, but Rick easily blocked the blows and kneed him in the sternum. As Ash doubled over in pain, heaving, Rick realized he had gone too far and had a flashback to his childhood; his father was an abusive drunk and would beat him for stepping out of line in the slightest way. His mother was of no help, although loving, but would not interfere, out of fear that he'd also turn on her.

Rick often attributed his childhood trauma to be the sole cause of his never trying to settle down and start a family; he thought things would be different once he found Ash. He knew from firsthand experience how damaging something like this could be to a child, and how it can linger for years to come, always eating away at them as they never felt like they were good enough. He felt a wave of embarrassment come over him and turned to walk away, stepping in front of the window to gather himself.

He stared outside at the ground, with the shame of what he'd just done flowing through him. He was surprised at how easy and natural it came to him, and made the conscious choice to stop blaming his father and take the brunt of the blame, for in this moment he was an adult, and of his own volition harmed his most valued companion. The guilt immediately began gnawing at him, and he made an internal promise to himself that his hands would never hurt Ash again. As he turned around to apologize he noticed that Ash was no longer bent over, he was standing, head tilted down, hair awry and partially covering his face.

Rick tried to apologize, "Look, Ash. I'm so—".

"Shut up! I'll kill you!"

As he stood up tall and peered into Rick's eyes with hatred, the man noticed that Ash looked more intimidating than ever. Ash's eyes turned a shade of purple and had a slight glow about them. He was seething, clenching his fists and breathing heavily. As he opened his fists, what appeared to be purple lightning began arcing around his fingers.

Ash could see the fear in Rick's eyes, as the man took a step back, butted up against the window frame. He looked at the boy as if he was some sort of monster, a beast about to strike him down. Ash was reveling in this moment, he knew that he would make Rick pay for putting his hands on him and keeping him locked away like a prisoner.

He felt power coursing through him and with a push from deep down inside he released it. Thrusting his hands out towards Rick, and with a guttural scream, he shot purple lightning out of his hands, striking the man in the chest and sending him tumbling through the window where he fell two stories before landing in a pile of filled trash bags.

Ash, confused about what had happened, looked down at his hands, inspecting them. He thought to himself that it couldn't be real, normal people can't just shoot lightning out of their hands, could they? Freaking out, he ran out of the apartment, downstairs, and around the building where Rick lay.

Running up to him, he dove onto his body, frantically checking his neck for a pulse. He was screaming in his head, *please don't be dead, please don't be dead!* The pulse was confirmed; Ash let loose a sigh of relief, very thankful he wasn't a teen murderer. He found Rick's cell phone and dialed 911, explaining that he'd found an injured man, gave them the address, and hung up. As guilty as he felt, Ash realized this was the moment he was waiting for, now was the time for him to escape.

Ash ran back upstairs to the apartment, looking around for anything he may want to take with him before remembering he owned virtually nothing, and dashed back downstairs. He exited the building, looking like any normal teenage boy with his red and blue jacket, blue jeans, and dirty Converse shoes. Ash ran with tears streaming down his face. There were times when Ash wished that Rick would have just walked passed him on the night he was found, not because Rick was bad to him, but because of how he was made to live. He wondered if Rick felt the same way and assumed at this moment he did for sure.

Ash slowed to a brisk walk, breathing hard and wiping his face; while catching his breath he looked back over his shoulder to make sure he wasn't being followed by the police. He saw no one but as he turned back around he noticed a girl roughly twenty yards away watching him intently.

She was a pretty girl with blond hair long enough to go past her shoulders. She had piercing blue eyes which had a hue Ash had never seen before, almost as if they bore a slight glow. She was wearing blue jeans, a light blue T-shirt, and a denim jacket.

Her hands wore black gloves with missing fingertips. The girl couldn't have been much older than Ash and was roughly the same height, maybe even slightly shorter. He noted that he found her to be very pretty, but was worried about the way she was watching him. The thing that bothered him the most was how familiar she looked, although he knew he had never met her before, or any girl for that matter. Ash looked over his shoulder again and when he turned back to look at the girl, she was gone.

As Ash rounded the corner of a building the girl appeared, seemingly out of thin air. Caught by surprise he opened his mouth to scream but before he could she covered his mouth with one of her gloved hands. She said, "Don't draw any attention to us. You're being followed and you need to come with me if you want to survive."

Ash felt a buzzing in his stomach, he had never had a girl touch him before and she was very pretty after all. Again, the familiarity with this girl is what made him decide to follow along, however, he was skeptical.

"Hey wait. Who are you? Who's after me? Where are we going?"

"Listen, I don't have time to explain all of this to you right now. I just need you to trust me."

She grabbed his wrist and began to pull him along, but he yanked away from her grip and paused. "I'm not going anywhere until I get some answers."

Noticing his resolve, the girl said "Okay fine, I'll give you some of the answers, but we have to keep walking."

Ash followed her as she turned away and began walking at a fast pace. He saw her pull something silver from her pocket and blow into it but no sound came out. She said, "My name is Quinn Avery. I'm taking you back to a place called Asmaria. I've been sent to find you. The people after you belong to a group called The Forbidden; we don't know a whole lot about them other than the fact that they want to destroy Asmaria and its people. Anyone who has ever tried to infiltrate them to find answers hasn't returned. The rest will have to wait. We have to hurry, we don't have much time."

"Well that didn't clear up much, but it's better than nothing I guess. So what do these guys want with me, and how did you know what happened in my apartment?"

"Like I said I can't exp- ah!"

Just then two men appeared in front of the young duo. One of the men was massive; he towered over the kids and was noticeably very muscular through his clothes. He was bald and had a scar running diagonally from the left side of his forehead, all the way down to the right side of his chin. He was smiling with teeth that looked like they belonged to some sort of wild beast. The other man was shorter. He had a clean haircut with black hair; the only feature that stood out to Ash was a prominent mustache that any man would be proud of. He found it odd that they were wearing matching outfits. The pair wore black combat boots, black leather pants, a black v-neck t-shirt, and a black trench coat. They both had an arrogant bravado about them that didn't go unnoticed by Ash.

"Who are you creeps and what do you want?" Ash tried to make himself appear taller and more threatening.

The bigger of the two men chuckled, and said in a deep voice almost like a growl, "Ah, where are my manners? My name is Balthazar and this is my colleague, Blaize." The man named Blaize said nothing but gave a slight nod. "We'd like you to come with us."

"And why would I want to do that?"

Using the conversation as a distraction, Quinn summoned putrid water from a nearby sewage drain, using a sweeping motion with her hands, and then thrust them forward, blasting both of the men with the nasty liquid with a force that sent them flying several feet away and landing on their backs. "Run!" She grabbed Ash by the hand, who was in awe of what he just witnessed, and began pulling him along behind her as she ran.

They ran together past the sopping wet goons who bellowed with rage, spitting curses at the two kids as they fled. Quinn hauled Ash up a large hill, not stopping until they had reached the top. He looked back in the direction they'd come to check for their pursuers, saw nothing, and then noticed how beautiful the New York skyline appeared.

"Now what?" he wheezed as he stood there breathing heavily.

"Just wait, it should be here soon." Quinn was breathing perfectly fine as if she was used to this sort of thing.

Ash noticed a small shape appear in the sky. He was not able to make out what it was, but as it got closer he noticed flapping wings. He began to panic, thinking it was a monster of some sort. Some other fiend the girl had forgotten to mention to him, another foe coming to try to end his life. As they stood there the thing came closer and he realized that it was a bird resembling an eagle. The problem was that it seemed too big to be real. It was a large bird with a wingspan that had to be at least fifteen feet across.

His legs began to shake, but Quinn said, "Put your hand in the air and make a fist!" He did as she said apprehensively and the massive bird swooped down, grabbing them each around the wrist with its talons. As the bird flew away Ash turned towards the hill only to see the two men from before moving with incredible speed up the hill.

Quinn effortlessly climbed up and onto the back of the giant eagle and then helped Ash up as well. After getting up to the bird's back he noticed how exhausted his body was. He promptly passed out, not caring what would come next.

Ash awoke and was surprised to see that they were still flying. The ocean and the sky around them looked amazing. This is what Ash had always wanted to see, the world.

"How long was I out for?"

"It's been about three hours I'd say. We're getting close to Asmaria."

"What exactly is Asmaria anyway?"

"Oh right. It's an island that has remained hidden from the normal human population for thousands of years."

Ash looked around but saw only water for as far as he could see."Okay, and what is so special about this place? Why are you taking me there? Also, I feel like I know you from somewhere which is impossible because I've never talked to you or any other girl for that matter."

Realizing what he just said, Ash blushed with embarrassment. He silently chastised himself for being so dumb.

Quinn smirked and giggled, "There is so much to explain and not enough time to do it. The Guardians will have to fill you in on most of it. They're in charge of the Guild."

"Okay. You just said a lot of words and I'm confused even more. How did you know my name by the way? I didn't tell you that."

"To put it in simple terms the Guild is an organization of mages that I am a member of. We have our meetings at a place called the Capitol which is located on the island of Asmaria. You see, on Asmaria, not everyone is born with a special ability.

Those of us who are will train our entire lives to be warriors for Asmaria. The reason I seem familiar and the reason why I know so much about you is because you're an Asmarian. We're drawn to each other, and our parents used to be friends, or so my mom told me."

"Wait, you know my parents?"

"No. I never met them myself. No one has seen or heard from your parents since the night you were abandoned eleven years ago. The Guardians will have to tell you more about it." She saw his hopes drop by the sullen look on his face, "I'm sorry."

"Not your fault," he responded morosely.

Ash was no stranger to pain or disappointment. That small glimmer of hope he had when Quinn mentioned his parents faded just as quickly as it appeared.

"This is a lot to process."

Quinn took his hand in hers and he felt his face get hot again. They looked at each other and she smiled, but he didn't smile back. He pulled his hand free, not because he wasn't grateful for it, but because it was hard for him to trust anyone. Quinn looked a little hurt, but the feeling passed.

Ash was very curious, and surprised it took him so long to mention it, "So what's with the massive bird?"

"Oh, this is one of our giant eagles, Reginald."

"Reginald?" he laughed, which resulted in a loud cry from the bird, confirming this was indeed his name.

"Wait, what do you mean *one* of your giant eagles?"

"Well, Asmaria is different from anything you've ever experienced before. We have all sorts of creatures. Some are different versions of animals you'd recognize, and some, well… you'll just have to see for yourself."

Ash felt Reginald slowing down as he looked out across the horizon. He could see an island closing in and noticed that Asmaria wasn't all that large. From the air, he could see a lot of forestation and big blooming flowers. Some small rivers cut through the landscape here and there. He could see a bright glowing city not far from where they appeared to be landing. The sun was setting, casting orange and pink streaks across the sky. As they came closer to the island he could see a circular platform extending from a cliff hanging over the sea, almost like a helipad, with four individuals on it. They wore exquisite attire, but something was off about it that Ash couldn't quite place from this distance. It almost seemed to be alive, and they each had their color scheme which included blue, orange, green, and white.

As they got closer he was able to see the finer details of their clothing. Each seemed to be made from an element. The small woman in blue appeared to be surrounded by a flowing dress of royal blue water. A bronze-skinned man dressed in green was covered with mossy, shifting earth. The tall man in the middle was ablaze, his garments writhing with dancing orange flames. On the far right in white stood another woman, taller than the last but shorter than the men, whose dress was iridescent. Hers was the most difficult for Ash to figure out. The thing that caught Ash's attention the most though, was their eyes. Each person had a soft glow to their eyes that matched the color of the clothing they were wearing.

The two kids dismounted Reginald as the man in orange stepped forward, and with a deep, booming voice, "Welcome to Asmaria Ash. We have much to discuss. Quinn my dear, run into any trouble out there?"

"None that I couldn't handle sir." She gave a small curtsy.

Ash could tell from how she carried herself around him that he was important.

The woman in blue stepped forward saying, "Now then, let us adjourn to the Capitol immediately. We must attend to business before the feast."

Ash perked up, feeling his tummy rumble, "Feast? Thank goodness, I'm starving!"

Paradise In The Pit

Somewhere dark, under the ground, where only a few knew the location, Blaize and Balthazar were being berated by their comrades for not capturing the children. Blaize was furious; he had been stuck with this oaf for the past several years. *It's not my fault that the ways of shadow do not come naturally to me, why should I be stuck with this moron?* he often thought to himself. Apart from not being gifted with powers, Blaize was a formidable soldier. His skills with fighting were surpassed by very few others in the Forbidden.

He was generally well-liked by his friends until the two brats in New York ruined his image. He didn't understand what the big deal with them was; sure, the boy was supposed to be the one of prophecy, but he didn't believe in that old myth anyway. That girl though, no one warned them that the boy would have friends with him. They went under-prepared and the results were clear evidence of this. Blaize thought that this was all a plot to get them into trouble again; often they would be on the receiving end of a beating from the other Forbidden, however, Blaize didn't receive much of the bruising. This happened most often because Balthazar dropped the ball with something important.

They stood in the middle of the foyer of their lair, the Pit, as other members of their brotherhood circled them, shouting insults. They were pelted with rocks and scraps of food until in walked Ozul, their fearless leader, with his mask which he never took off. He shouted over the noise, "Silence!"

The yelling immediately died down and the sea of bodies split as he approached, walking slowly towards the two failures. He circled them, like a shark in the ocean when it smelled blood and found its prey. Ozul usually just gave them a slap on the wrist for their shortcomings which equated to a few days in the dungeon where they had to fight off the horrific beasts there. They always came out alive, but never unscathed.

Ozul, with venom in his words, said, "You two have failed me for the last time." He paused and then addressed the rest of the crowd, "Let this be a clear message to the rest of you, failure of any kind, from this point forth will not be tolerated!"

Blaize trembled, scared for the first time in a while. Usually, Lord Ozul was more restrained. He rarely lashed out at them apart from issuing their sentence to the dungeons or whatever punishment he'd come up with. Blaize hadn't seen him this angry at them in a long time.

Two giant, shadowy hands erupted from the ground beneath them and clasped around Balthazar and Blaize's throats, lifting them a foot off the ground, their feet kicking wildly. They choked and sputtered, clawing at the choking force, but it did no good. Blaize saw spots in his vision and as he felt his consciousness slip, the hands dropped them both to the floor. He watched Ozul pace back and forth in front of them, as they fought for air.

"Please master," Balthazar grumbled, "it won't happen again. I swear! I'm begging you, spare us, have mercy!"

Blaize just looked at him with disgust.

Ozul threw his head back and laughed, "Mercy? *Me* give you mercy? No, that simply won't do. You must be punished!"

"Just kill us already then!" said Blaize. He couldn't stand it anymore. He hated his life here; he was born in the caves and grew up barely surviving on the scraps of food that were provided. It was no way to live, but what was he supposed to do? He accepted it just as everyone else did, but he seemed to be the only one who hated being part of this evil organization. He just wanted it to be over with.

Ozul knelt slowly, using his index finger to lift Blaize's chin, making him stare into that emotionless masked face. "No one has ever spoken to me in such a manner. It may not seem like it, but I've never had this much respect for you."

Blaize thought that maybe he would be forgiven, but the thought was short-lived. Ozul stood back up, grabbed each of the men with shadowy tentacles, and stood them back up to their feet. He held their bodies in place and then produced another tendril to wrap around their heads. He made a violent twisting motion with his hands, their heads were twisted 90 degrees to the rear. Bones crunching and tendons popping could be heard as their necks were broken, killing them instantly.

Ozul dragged their bodies across the gravelly floor of the cave with his shadows. He wrenched open the steel door that held the beasts behind it at bay. The smell of rancid, rotted flesh spewed out. Loud enough for everyone to hear he said, "Let this be a lesson to you all. From here on out, I will feed you to the karnigrots alive. I've shown mercy to these two by ending their lives first."

He allowed the door to stay open long enough for the people

to look in and see the large creatures with their furry bodies, long claws, and saliva dripping from their fangs. Their serpent tails whipped side-to-side with excitement.

Ozul tossed the bodies inside and slammed the door shut as the beasts pounced on their meal. He could hear the snarling and crunching as the karnigrots devoured the feast. He felt that his warning to the others went well.

Ozul made his way back to the throne room where his master resided, he walked slowly, fearful for what was to come next. He knew there would be repercussions for an unsuccessful mission. Ozul believed that capturing the boy would be simple, so simple that even the two lowest-ranking members could accomplish it. He bashed himself for not going to make sure everything went smoothly.

He opened the door and his dark lord sat on his throne, waiting for him to enter. The shady figure sat with his hands together, fingers interlaced, yellow eyes menacingly watching his underling approach. His footsteps echoed in the chamber as his feet slapped the cold, sweating floor. A few feet away from the fiery throne, Ozul knelt, "My lord, I-" but before he could finish he was flung across the room.

His head smacked the obelisk, which was the source of all their power, in the center of the chamber, and he felt woozy. A lump already formed by the time he felt his head with his fingers, he pulled them away, slick with blood. Ozul dared not stand back up, he simply went into a turtle position on the ground, bowing in submission.

That low, enticing voice echoed throughout the room, bouncing off the rocky walls, "I told you to bring me the boy. Tell me, why does he not enter with you?"

"He got away, my lord."

"Yes, yes, I know. I see everything, remember? How is it he was able to slip from your grasp?"

"I sent someone else."

"Oh you did, did you? Well," he grinned evilly, "now you get to pay for their mistakes."

"But my lord, I already disposed of them. They were useless anyway. I know I must be punished, but I beg of you, have a little mercy on your humble servant."

"Disposed of them? You dwindled our already sparse numbers in hopes that I would spare your life?"

Ozul shuddered, he never thought that killing off those morons would be seen as a bad thing to anyone. "I'm sorry, master."

"Yes, well, I'm not going to kill you. Not yet anyway."

Relief melted the fear coursing through Ozul's body. He wasn't going to kill him, he lived to serve his master another day. "Thank you, my lord."

"Oh, I wouldn't thank me just yet."

The dark lord stood from his throne and using his mind, took control of Ozul. He lifted him off the ground and flung him up into the ceiling with a lot of force. Ozul was sure that a couple of ribs were broken as he smashed the rocks above, the breath knocked from his lungs. He fell back down to the ground and landed flat on his belly. The master held him there flat and sauntered over. He reached into the air and fashioned a small blade out of the darkness.

Ozul's coat and shirt were sliced down the middle, exposing his skin to the cool air. His master began carving his name into the man's bare flesh, resulting in muffled screams coming from the victim. The process was slow and excruciating, the demon reveled in the anguish of his minion.

When all was done, and Ozul was allowed to leave, he went back to his quarters. He took the rest of his clothes off and walked over to his wall mirror. Turning his back to it, he saw that the message, carved in bloody letters, read his master's name, AROS.

Asmaria

The group of Asmarians began walking away, down some steps that resembled clouds. Ash hesitated to step on the first one for fear of falling through, but after seeing the others take the lead he went for it. They were fluffy, just as he imagined they would be, but they didn't budge. Ash looked around taking in all the beauty. The cloudy stairs led to a lush forest with the prettiest trees and flowers that Ash had ever seen. He wasn't sure this was even real.

As they walked, Ash posed a question, "So, is anyone going to explain all this to me or what?"

He saw Quinn startle and say, "Ash! Watch how you speak to the Guardians! They're the four most powerful mages in Asmaria, they deserve respect."

"HA! No need to worry yourself, Quinn." The Guardian in orange replied with a hearty laugh. "My name is Brandr. I'm essentially the leader of the Guardians, although I don't like to think of myself that way. I'd prefer that we are all thought of as equal, but Asmarians do not change their customs easily. You may address us by name or just say, sir or ma'am."

"Don't call me by my name."

The man in green looked annoyed as if he was having a bad day, but Ash figured he was like this more often than not. He had his arms folded as they walked.

Well someone seems grumpy, Ash thought.

"That one there is Avani. Don't worry, his bark is worse than his bite," said Brandr who received a squint-eyed sneer from the disgruntled Avani.

The woman in blue spoke up with a voice that Ash thought was too high for an adult, "It's a pleasure to finally meet you, Ash. My name is Leena, I'm a water mage in case you couldn't tell from the clothes."

Ash replied, "Oh about that. What's with the fancy get-up?"

"Well, when you become one of the Guardians you receive a specially made uniform for you to wear while on duty. We don't always wear these, but they do make a great first impression right?" Leena seemed incredibly upbeat and jovial.

"You've got that right."

The other woman spoke up, "Hi, my name is Bora. I'm a wind mage. We Guardians each have one element that we specialize in."

Bora wore iridescent white clothes, which made sense to Ash that she was the wind mage. He deduced that Avani was an earth mage even though the man didn't care to tell him so. As he was taking this all in he noticed there was no Guardian of lightning.

Stymied, he asked, "So I don't know if you all know this, but I zapped my adoptive father with some sort of lightning, and I couldn't help but notice you guys didn't mention lightning."

The Guardians did not show any sort of surprise or recognition that this was news to them. Brandr spoke more quietly than before, "We are well aware of what transpired at your home in New York. You will learn more about the Great Tree later but for now, I will tell you that She has given me many visions regarding you. We couldn't interfere with your growth in fear that your powers may have never manifested. Everything happens for a reason, my friend.

"Asmarian mages develop powers at different ages, although, for most of us it happens between ten and fifteen years old. We had to wait for your abilities to manifest, in fear that if we stepped in you would have never developed. There is not anyone alive today who has met a lightning wielder, but more of you may have existed in the past. We have a long and complicated history. We aren't sure how those goons know about you, but we will get to the bottom of it."

Visions? Talking trees? Ash was becoming confused. This along with the knowledge that these people knew about him and his situation and elected to do nothing made anger surge through him.

A swell of rage built up inside of him. His eyes began to electrify with purple lightning. He felt a surge of power course through his veins as his fingertips began to tingle. Before Ash could release the build-up of energy he suddenly found himself encased in dirt up to his neck. The power faded and his breathing slowed; looking at Avani, he noticed the man was holding his hands clasped together, and the dirt surrounding him had a tight grip.

"I'm sorry. I don't know what happened," Ash said.

"It's natural to feel angry over what you just heard Ash. But please try to understand, we would have come for you sooner, but had we done so, your powers may have never appeared." Brandr pleaded. "We believe in fate, and that it was fate that put you in the arms of Rick. Had we interfered, I think your outcome would have been much different. We face a great evil in our world and you will be the one that brings balance, I firmly believe that. Fear not my boy, with time and practice you will learn to control your power."

Ash decided to let it go. "Okay, I understand. Can you let me go now?"

With a grunt, Avani released the earthen hold he had on the boy. Ash was still processing everything he'd just heard.

A pang of guilt tore through Ash. He hadn't thought of Rick since he took off from the apartment. It was only now, when Brandr mentioned him, that Ash remembered what he'd done to his dad. He wondered how he could be so heartless to not even worry about Rick's well-being. But he was concerned now that things had slowed down, so maybe he wasn't so bad after all.

Ash asked, "Is there any way that we can check on Rick? I'm worried about him. After I.. ya know."

Brandr said, "We already sent a scout to locate him. He was nowhere to be found. I'm sorry."

Ash's head hung low and he fought back tears. He didn't want anyone to see him cry so he choked the sadness back down. "Nothing we can do about it now. I just hope he's okay."

After emerging from the forest, which seemed to go on forever, Ash could see a thriving city. The buildings were taller than anything he had ever seen, granted he had never been outside of Rick's apartment until now. They were all different colors. Some seemed to be built of jade, which he imagined would shimmer brightly in the sun. The city was lit by other buildings that were ablaze in fire. Most of them were constructed from one of the elements which made them seem alive as their surfaces shifted. Normally this would cause concern in people, but it seemed to be everyday life for the Asmarians. The city didn't appear to be very big, but it was bustling with foot traffic. The Capitol wasn't very modern; no vehicles could be seen, or street lamps. Ash wondered if they had wi-fi.

Other mages were using their abilities to move around. Some were carrying themselves across the land with gusts of wind. Those who controlled the earth were being carried along effortlessly. He saw no water or fire mages flitting about, but that made sense to him. It would be difficult to propel yourself with those.

This was stunning for Ash, he had never seen such vibrant colors or awe-inspiring abilities before. The people with no magic walked along at a snail's pace compared to the mages whooshing by them, but they seemed happy.

The people on the street were quick to notice the group making their way through the city. They stopped to stare, wondering who this foreigner was. Ash never had anyone take notice of him like this before and he didn't like it. He felt static in his hands and forced himself to calm down.

Soon enough they reached a smaller building close to the center of the Capitol. It was only a couple of stories tall and was circular. The outside was painted in a solid gray color, nothing too special about it. Maybe they wanted it to be inconspicuous.

Brandr, startled Ash from his deep thought, "This is where the Guild meets, although we won't have the entire group show up just yet, first thing tomorrow morning we must meet with all the mages. For now, let us give you some answers, and then we eat!"

They walked into the building and Ash noticed that it looked pretty normal inside as well, not built with the same loudness as the other buildings. The front door opened up into an atrium with short ceilings. Past that was a long corridor that wrapped around the inner edge of the building. The only decorations were rows and rows of painted pictures containing every Guardian in the past and ending with the current group. The considerable hallway led to tall double doors made of wood that resembled a Nordic cherry. They went through the doors into a massive auditorium with many rows of seats.

Kinda looks like the Roman coliseum.

"Wow, this place is huge!" Ash exclaimed.

Chuckling, Brandr motioned for them to sit at the long wooden table in the center of the arena floor. "Now then, let's get down to business. I'll tell you everything I know of your life up until this point. How does that sound, Ash?"

"Sounds great. Let's start with my real parents."

Brandr had a grim look on his face as he explained, "Well, I knew both of your parents. They were very highly ranked within the Guild. They were very powerful mages, your father was a fire user and your mother harnessed water. Your father's name was Augustus and your mother, Iris. Together they were formidable. Augustus was rugged and strong, Iris gentle and loving.

"One night they left together with you in tow—you were only a year old—without telling anyone and didn't show up for the next meeting. We began the search, looking everywhere on the island at first and then expanding past it. There was no sign of them, until.." his expression darkened further, "until we found her body. Iris had been murdered in the land that you came from. You were alone, beside her corpse with no sign of your father anywhere." Brandr had tears welling in his eyes while telling this story.

He continued, "The scout we sent picked you up and laid you on that park bench to be found. Again, the Great Tree told us what to do. As hard as it was, we wanted to protect you from further tragedy. We brought Iris home and gave her a proper mage's burial. Being put to rest with the Great Tree is an honor for our people. Your father hasn't been seen since then."

Ash took in this information, letting it all soak in. He was hit with a wave of emotion and everyone felt static move from him, around the table, and through all sitting there. It subsided as he calmed himself down.

"So, tell me more about this tree. Is my mom still buried there? Can I go see her?"

Leena responded, "Oh, I'll take this one. The Great Tree is at the very center of the island. The Guardians visit the Tree often and gain guidance from it. We have learned over the years that this is where all of the magic in Asmaria comes from. It's a sacred place. When one of us dies we must be buried near the roots of the tree so that our life force can be transferred to the tree, keeping it sustained. Your mother has long been absorbed by the Great Tree."

Ash thought that sounded weird but said, "I'd like to go see it sometime anyway if that's okay."

"Of course. We can do that very soon, but not tonight."

"So Brandr, why have I never heard of Asmaria before now? And are there any other powers that you guys have, or other elements that people have been able to control?"

"Asmarians have been very skilled at hiding the island from the outside world since the very beginning. People from other places also seem to be far more skeptical, it's as if their disbelief in all things mystical disallows them from finding our island. Some have ventured close, but we never let them reach our beaches."

Brandr paused for a moment, considering how to answer

the second question, and then went on, "Regarding those with other abilities, I have never met anyone in my lifetime that can control another element, except for The Forbidden. They have a peculiar kind of magic, being able to manipulate shadows and take control of darkness itself."

As Ash was mulling over this overload of information Bora interjected, "Okay I'm starving and I'm sure Ash is too. Let's go eat!"

"Absolutely!" Ash responded excitedly.

"To the Field of Bliss! It's a beautiful area where we have special ceremonies. Tonight we will have a large fire and celebrate the return of our long-lost Asmarian!"

Enveloped In Darkness

After leaving the Guild building they walked down more cobblestone streets passing the beautiful, magical architecture. Buildings swirling with waves, writhing with flames, shifting earth, or others that looked like clouds moving through the sky, being pushed by the wind. Past the city there were more trees, luckily there was a path for them to follow that was lit by torches. No one spoke as they trudged through the forest, the only sounds to be heard were the footfalls of the group and the nightlife in the forest around them. Ash saw a firefly land on Brandr's shoulder and thought it was ironic.

The forest opened up into a large field encircled by more torches. The moon glowed overhead and there was a slight breeze, but it felt nice outside. Ash noticed that there were others already gathered there, more mages playing with their abilities calmly. They were dressed in clothing that he assumed belonged to the color of their ability. It was different from the Guardians, their attire seemed halfway normal and didn't shift with an element as the leader's did. They surrounded a fire that seemed to be burning nothing. He saw no wood or anything combustible in the flames. It was simply burning the air.

Brandr startled a few of those gathered with his booming

voice, "Welcome all to our celebration of our abandoned Asmarian reunited with the homeland. His name is Ash, and he has traveled a far distance so let's give him a great Asmarian welcome!"

Applause, along with hoots and hollers erupted from the crowd of mages. As they became silent once again, food platters seemed to float in from the trail behind them. Upon closer inspection, Ash noticed small fairy-looking creatures were bringing the dishes in.

"What the heck?" he said to no one in particular but received a few chuckles anyway.

Quinn leaned in and whispered, "Those are the elemental spirits that help us keep this place going. Without them, Asmaria wouldn't be nearly as amazing. Each one represents one of the four main elements. They don't mind helping us with our gatherings and other chores, so long as we give them plenty of island sugar to eat."

Ash was awestruck by what he was seeing. The spirits brought in tables and chairs, goblets of drink, dishes of food, anything he could imagine was there. Everyone sat down once the tiny flying creatures flew away and began to dine. Ash was ravenous as he sat at a circular table with the four Guardians and Quinn. He thought how good she looked with her face lit up by the fire. His cheeks burned when she caught him staring and she let out a small giggle as he turned his eyes back to his food.

The table was engaged in conversation, most of it was Ash asking questions about his powers, but they didn't seem to know a whole lot. Ash could hear the other tables laughing and joking with each other. He was finally happy, all he ever wanted was to see the outside world, but Rick just couldn't let him go.

Peering into the flames of the fire at the center of the clearing, Ash couldn't help but wonder what his parents would have been like had he grown up with them. The fire was casting shadows that seemed to dance. It appeared as if the fire was beginning to fade when suddenly it exploded, sending sparks into the air, and casting a large shadow that was shaped like a human.

The gathered mages let loose a cry of surprise, flying from their seats they formed battle positions, ready for whatever was coming their way. The shadow looked fairly tall and was wearing a hooded cloak. It was impossible to make out any facial features. The guardians formed a small tight circle around Ash and Quinn. They lifted their hands which glowed with the magic of each respective element. Their eyes glowed brighter than before. Brandr sent a concentrated blast of fire from his palm, striking the shadowy figure in the chest where his heart would be, but it just passed right through him. It narrowly missed a mage who was behind the shadow.

In a garbled voice that barely sounded human, the shadow spoke, "Calm down you puny ants. This is just one of my many abilities, shadow projection, you can't hurt me while in this form. Most of you aren't worth my time and energy anyway, however, there is one among you who has caught my attention. I want to speak with the one known as Ash."

Ash, brandishing as much confidence as he could muster even though he was terrified, slowly stepped around the guardians into the view of the shadow.

"Ah, there you are. You're a tough one to track down." His posture was relaxed and he sounded happy to have found Ash.

"Who are you, and what do you want with me?" Ash snapped the words at the dark figure, trying to sound menacing.

The man responded with a growl, "Watch your tone with me, boy. I am Ozul, master of the Forbidden." Ash felt his tone calm, almost soothing as he said, "Join me, Ash. I will make you more powerful than you could ever imagine. You will be part of our brotherhood, never alone again. You will join our family and together we will do great things."

"Let me think. Umm, no thanks. Now get lost before I get upset."

"I'm going to give you the benefit of the doubt and pretend like I didn't hear that. I'll give you one month to reconsider my offer. You will meet me at the park in which you were found as a baby, Birkwood Park. Then, you will join me, otherwise, I will murder your father while you watch."

With that, Ozul waived his arm and another shadow appeared next to him; the new apparition resembled a man bound and gagged groaning in desperation. "You have one month, Ash." And with that final sentence, the shadows disappeared just as quickly as they came.

Ash was completely silent with shock. He had no idea how to respond to what just happened. His father? His real father has been captive this whole time? If this were true, he had to do whatever he could to save him. He looked to Brandr, waiting for a response.

Brandr said, "I have no idea how he knew so much about you, but now we know why those two goons were after you. It's clear they know something we don't and want you to be part of their organization. Ash, you have to believe me when I say I had no idea they had your father. If we had suspected he was alive we would have attempted a rescue long ago."

Bora interjected, "We shall discuss this more tomorrow, for now, Quinn my dear, show Ash to his new home."

"Yes ma'am."

Quinn grabbed Ash by the wrist and dragged him along, back toward the way they had come. He could hear the conversations of the other mages as they walked away.

Ash didn't know how to react to everything that happened within the past 24 hours and looked for comfort in Quinn, "I'm so confused right now, I have no idea what to make of everything that's happened. I just want to go to sleep and wake up back in my apartment in New York tomorrow like nothing happened."

"I know, but just stick it out and it will all make more sense soon, I'm sure of it."

He said, "What makes you so sure?"

She paused and then said, "Everything works out the way it's supposed to. When I was tasked to come find you in New York, I had to blend it. The city was scary. There were tons of people and vehicles. I don't know if you've noticed but Asmarians live a more humble lifestyle. And then I had to wear these, no offense, goofy clothes."

Her grin gave Ash butterflies.

The thought of the clothes he'd grown up wearing being weird to someone made him chuckle."Yeah, I understand. When do I get my cool mage outfit?"

"We can go get you some tomorrow maybe. Just depends on what the Guardians have planned for us. I think there will be a Guild meeting as well, considering recent events, so that should be fun."

They walked together through the forest and back down the streets of the city until they came to a row of identical homes on the outskirts. They were all made of stone and had the same design, although the sizes were a bit different. Ash was surprised that it didn't look as glamorous as the rest of the city.

Quinn led him to one of the small houses, gesturing with her hand, "Well this is my house. It's late, otherwise, I'd introduce you to my parents, but you can meet them tomorrow. That house two doors down from mine is yours. All to yourself, which is why it's a little smaller. I'll see you tomorrow, goodnight."

"Goodnight. Oh, and Quinn?"

"Yeah?"

"Thanks for being so cool to me today."

She smiled widely, "No problem."

With that, she quietly went inside and Ash headed to his new home. Looking at the house he saw there were two windows on either side of the front door. The stone of the house was different colors, brown, red, green, and even some black in there. Entering into the house he noticed a few things; it seemed very similar to how any normal house would look, but the fireplace had a series of buttons next to it. He walked over to investigate further and pressed the on switch causing a blaze to appear. With the buttons, he was able to change the intensity and the color to anything he wanted. The entire appeared to be opened up to reveal the sky, but when he stood on a chair to try touching it there was a connection. Ash just assumed that it was some sort of visual trickery going on there.

Ash decided he wanted a quick shower before passing out. He found the bathroom and discovered the shower was amazing. He took his clothes off and hopped in, turning the water on, and was blasted from every direction. He took a quick, hot shower, and got out smelling and feeling fresh. He didn't have the energy to do much else so he promptly dove into the bed, which was soft and plushy, softer than anything he'd ever experienced.

He sank into the pillows without having the strength to even climb under the blanket, within seconds he was out.

42

Kane

Kane Volorium was born into one of the wealthier families of Asmaria, he'd grown up with the proverbial silver spoon in his mouth. He came from a long line of powerful water mages, so it was a big shock when he conjured wind for the first time, carrying a paper airplane across a large room, making it fly in big arcing loops as if it had a mind of its own. Shortly after that, he left the academy that all Asmarian children start in and went to the train with the Guild.

A lot of his family resented him for being different from the rest of his bloodline, but his parents were very supportive of him. If that didn't make him stand out enough, he was also born with bright, white hair.

He was teased over his hair, despite his sharp jawline and blue eyes. He took a positive outlook on life rather than letting it get to him. He loved his white hair and embraced it; to him, it was just another sign that he was special. Kane had big plans for his future; he wanted to become the strongest mage in history, stronger than any of the Guardians, past and present. These were big shoes to fill, he knew that, but once he set his mind to something there was no turning back.

He trained every single day, only ever taking time off due to injury or when mandated by a superior. Kane loved practicing the throwing star, it was like an extension of him. Once he found his rhythm it didn't matter how far away he was. If he could put eyes on a target, he would hit his mark every time.

One day before training he wasn't watching where he was walking, lost in thought, he accidentally bumped into someone and knocked them down.

"Sorry!" He apologized frantically, "I didn't see you. My bad." He reached down to help the younger girl up.

"No problem. I wasn't paying attention either. My name's Quinn, what's yours?"

"Kane. Nice to meet you."

They shook hands and then made small talk for a minute. Quinn told him how much she struggled with her training; using magic didn't come easy for everyone and she was one of those that had trouble mastering it. Kane offered to help her out and she agreed.

Every day they would meet at the training field and practice their skills. Kane taught her how to use various weapons, nothing crazy just the basics. They'd practice their magic, having friendly duels. Sometimes Kane would let her win, just so she didn't get too discouraged. Before long a crush developed for Quinn; Kane thought she was very pretty, but he needed to stay focused on his goals. He knew that if he got sidetracked by girls then he'd never accomplish everything he wanted.

Over the years Kane had drifted away from Quinn. He was able to watch her develop into a stronger warrior as he did the same. He would see her at the training field or in Guild Meetings but they didn't talk much anymore.

The arrival of Ash to Asmaria was a bit of news to Kane, he was confused as to why he wasn't chosen to go on the rescue mission. He knew that Quinn was very strong, but she was also younger, and everyone knew that Kane was a prodigy. There wasn't a single weapon in their arsenal that he wasn't proficient with, and he gave everyone trouble with magic battles. The only wind mage he hadn't surpassed yet was Bora, and she was a Guardian so that's to be expected, although it still bugged him.

Jealousy struck him when he learned that he wasn't picked for this special mission; it wasn't often that Asmarians were sent to foreign lands, but he wanted to be picked for everything. Kane desperately yearned to be the guy that the Guardians turned to, he wanted to be the hero of Asmaria.

Kane, being very self-aware, realized these thoughts were only plaguing his progress and he couldn't afford to plateau; his father always told him that life was what you make it. Bad things happen to everyone and sometimes you don't get your way, but how you react to every situation is what makes it positive or negative. If your attitude is horrible, then the outcome of your problems will falter, but if you come at everything with positivity then things will usually work out in the end. And if they don't, just keep pressing forward.

Kane was always self-aware and tried to keep his emotions in check. He preferred to think of things from a logical standpoint, rather than emotional. He was briefly jealous of Quinn after learning that she was being sent to retrieve the long-lost Asmarian, but quickly let it go. He was excited to meet the kid and test his limits against him.

The Training Field

The day after arriving in Asmaria, Ash was woken up by the natural sunlight coming through the window above his bed. He slowly sat up and took a moment to take in his surroundings, and noticed the ceiling appeared to be normal now, painted an off-white color. The walls matched the ceiling and had no decorations apart from floating shelves scattering around. The bed was a full size which was bigger than what he was used to. The blanket was a light blue color and very soft. There was a closet and a dresser, one window above the bed, and that was it.

Ash climbed out of bed and walked into the kitchen which was also attached to a small living room area that had a couch and a couple of small chairs. His stomach rumbled loudly as he began to search for a snack, but his luck ran short when he found nothing. As he was putting his shoes on to go explore there was a knock at the door. Wondering who it could be, Ash rushed to the door, opening it to find a familiar face.

"Hey, sleepy head," Quinn said as he opened the door, squinting in the sunlight.

"Hey, where's a guy go to get some food around here?" He asked, stepping outside.

"Follow me, my mom has it covered. She's one of the best

cooks I know."

Ash followed her down the street to her house; the road they were on wasn't very busy, just a few small families milling about. He noticed something odd about them but couldn't quite put his finger on it.

Realizing what it was, he asked Quinn, "Hey, is it just me, or does no one around here have siblings?"

She looked down at her feet as she answered, "The people of Asmaria are only allowed to have one child per family. The only exception is if your child dies during childbirth." Ash was taken aback by this, it sounded strange.

Laughing, he said "You don't have to be embarrassed by that. I was beginning to think this place was too perfect. It's kind of refreshing, ya know?"

As they arrived at Quinn's house she opened the door and invited him inside. The smells alone made his stomach flip with excitement. On the couch, her father sat reading a book. He was short and stocky with short hair and a long bristly beard. With her back to the door stood Quinn's mom, making breakfast at the stove. Ash noticed that she had the same hair as Quinn.

Quinn's mom turned and said, "Hello dear, my name is Agatha, and this is my husband Ezra. It's so nice to meet you. Please come have a seat while I finish up in here." The man called Ezra did a small wave upon his introduction but said nothing and continued reading his book.

Agatha brought around a smorgasbord of food that, to Ash, looked just like an all-American breakfast. Eggs, bacon, biscuits, pancakes. Ash wondered how she did all that by herself. They all dug in, eating while asking Ash the occasional question about his childhood. After everyone became too full to take another bite, Ash and Quinn said their farewells and headed out the door.

"Where to now?" he asked.

"We need to go meet with the Guardians and see what they have planned for us today."

"Sounds like a plan to me. I'm excited to learn how to control my abilities. It seems like you're leagues ahead of me."

"Well, yeah I am," she said with a chuckle, "you have to remember, I've grown up around this stuff. I've trained very hard over the past couple of years to make sure I don't fall behind. It's only natural that I'd be a little better than you for right now."

"Yeah well, don't let that get to your head. I will catch up to you in no time!"

The two made their way down the street towards the Guild building making small talk. Once they entered the auditorium, Ash noticed that the Guardians were already in there speaking quietly. Before they could reach the table all the leaders stood up, noticing the kids, and walked towards them.

Brandr said, "Come with us, we have only a short time to get you ready to face Ozul. Your training must start at once."

Ash had completely forgotten about that deadline. A sense of fear washed over him. He wasn't strong enough to take on that guy by himself. He had a lot of growing to do and not much time to do it.

They walked out into the training field where there were people already training. He watched as mages practiced hand-to-hand combat, medical procedures, and magic wielding. There were targets of different sizes and shapes set up around the field, all made of metal to make them more durable.

They made their way through the field and Ash wondered

what his first training session would be like. They kept walking until they reached a little hut at the end of the field where Brandr knocked three times. Opening the door was a hunched-over, little old man with a long white beard.

"Ah, this is the boy eh? Well, come in, come in." the old man said with the most raspy of voices Ash had ever heard.

They all entered and Brandr said, "Ash this is Charlie. He is one of the oldest mages alive. He's going to teach you how to harness your power."

"Well, I like the sound of that."

Everyone left the hut except for Ash and Charlie, creating an awkward silence for just a moment, and then the old mage broke it, "I hear you can wield lightning. Never met someone who could do that before, although I doubt anyone has. Our people have been around for centuries, protecting this island and the Great Tree. Some aim to destroy it, thus killing all of our magic. We mustn't let them succeed. Now then, are you ready to get started?"

Ash nodded, "Let's do this gramps."

Chuckling, Charlie said, "Okay I'll show you how to conjure your power and talk you through it. First, close your eyes, and dig deep inside you with your mind, as if it has hands with which to grab the power inside you. Feel with your mind, the tendrils of power, and then grab it. Open your eyes and imagine that you're pushing the power with your mind down your arms and into your palms." Charlie did all of this while talking, producing a small, perfect sphere of water in each hand.

Ash began going through the steps he had just heard and saw the old man do. He closed his eyes and imagined he was searching for the lightning. He began to feel his mind buzzing with energy and latched onto it. He slowly opened his eyes, lifted his arms, palms facing the ceiling, and began pushing the energy down his arms and into his hands. Purple lighting began arcing in circles around his wrists, then his palms.

"Yes, that's it! That's it! Now, take control of it!"

"How do I take control of it?"

"The magic is a part of you. You have to imagine that you're pulling it into a ball from the inside of your hands. You can do it!"

Ash started to do as he was told, but doubt entered his mind. The arcs of lighting grew more wild and he panicked, sending a bolt directly toward his head. Ash fell to the floor, striking the back of his skull on the hard ground, darkness started closing in and he wondered if he would even wake up this time.

Awakening

Ash awoke with a start, sitting straight up in the hospital bed and startled Quinn who sat at his side. He looked around, noticing that it looked like a normal hospital. Quinn said, "How are you feeling? You've been out for two days. I was worried you were going to stay in the coma."

"I don't feel too bad, have a slight headache though." He laid back down, "What happened?"

"Well from what Charlie reported it sounds like you lost control and knocked yourself out."

"I'm never going to get the hang of this am I?"

"Of course you will. I have faith in you." She smiled, filling him with a warm feeling of gratitude.

Just then, a man wearing a white coat walked in, "I see you've woken up. My name is Dr. Landers, your vitals all look great. Here take a bite of this, it'll have you on your feet in no time." He handed Ash a small yellow square resembling a cookie.

"What is this?"

"It's called heala. It can cure anything. Just don't ask me what it's made of." He chuckled as he walked back out of the room. Ash though it tasted sort of like butterscotch. He scarfed it down and within an hour was feeling ready to go run a marathon. He was released from the infirmary and they made their way outside.

Quinn motioned for Ash to follow her and said, "I've been instructed to take you back to Charlie's hut."

Dread washed over him at the thought of knocking himself out again. "Ah man, do I have to do that today?"

"Look, I know it sucks that you got hurt the first time, but at this point, you only have 27 days left before your deadline. You need to be ready for battle."

"Yeah, you're right," he said with resolve, "This time I'll make sure to get the hang of it."

They walked in silence through the town except for. Ash couldn't help but notice how friendly everyone was. It was a strange place, some things like the hospital were exactly what he'd see on TV back home, it was like the Asmarians stuck to some sense of normalcy in the midst of being vastly unique. The city streets were so clean, compared to what he could remember seeing through the windows of the apartment in New York. A pang of guilt hit him as he remembered what he'd done to Rick. He told himself it was an accident and pushed it from his mind.

They approached the hut at the end of the training field and knocked. Opening the door, Charlie greeted them, "Hello again my young friend. Ready for round two?"

"Absolutely."

He said his goodbye to Quinn as she left the small shack.

"Okay, from the top, but this time try to remain confident. You have to *really* know that you're in control. Don't let the power control you, you own it, not the other way around."

Feeling a boost of confidence, Ash closed his eyes and started going through what he'd done the first time. Once the arcs of lightning appeared he focused in and reminded himself that he was the one in control. Slowly, he started pulling the arcs into little balls that vibrated at the center of his palms. The tendrils danced around but for the most part, had taken the shape he was going for.

Laughing and relieved, he said, "I did it! Now how do I make them go away without shooting them around the room?"

Charlie replied, "You're doing great! Now, what you want to do is imagine that you're severing a cord with scissors. Except the connection of power is the cord, and your mind is the scissors."

Doing his best, Ash closed his eyes and pictured a pair of shears cutting the connection of energy from his hands to his mind. The lightning dissipated and Ash felt relieved, and then he felt tired. He sat down on the floor rather hard sending a look of concern over the old man.

"Are you okay my boy?"

"I'm fine, I'm fine. Just need to rest for a minute."

After resting on the floor for a couple of minutes, he got up and Charlie told him that his training was complete and he was free to leave. Ash thanked him for everything and left the hut. Waiting for him in the center of the training field was Avani. Ash strode over to the frowning Guardian.

Avani grumbled, "Hurry up. I don't have all day."

Ash was taken aback by the brash statement and responded, "Ya know, everyone here is super nice to me. Except for you. Why is that? What did I ever do to you?"

This made the man's scowl worse as he responded, "Watch your tone with me, boy. I don't owe any explanation to you. Just know this, I don't trust you."

"Okay, noted. And right back at you."

With that, Avani motioned for Ash to follow him and so he

did. They came to a large, human-shaped target. There were other mages nearby that took notice of their arrival in this area. They stopped their training to see what was going on.

"Show me what you've got. Let's see what all the commotion over you is about. I don't think you've even got what it takes to be a Guild member, much less hit this target with anything significant."

Feeling his face get hot, Ash decided to show him what he's made of. He went through the steps that he'd learned to control the power. Forming balls of lightning in his hands, he realized that Charlie hadn't taught him how to shoot the energy out, only how to create and snuff it.

Embarrassed he said, "Um, I don't know how to shoot it."

Avani laughed with an air of cockiness, "Yeah some big shot you are. I guess if you can't figure it out on your own then you *really* don't deserve to be here."

Closing his eyes, Ash searched within himself for an answer. He opened his glowing purple eyes and mustered all the strength he could. With a scream he thrust both hands out towards the target, using his mind to push the lightning from his palms to the metal silhouette. Purple lightning surged into the metal with an intensity that surprised everyone watching, even Avani. The metal began to droop from being melted by the heat of the lightning. Ash released the lightning and almost fell again, but held his footing.

The crowd clapped in amazement, all except for Avani, whom Ash saw marching away from the training field. The onlookers closed in around Ash and clapped him on the back, each of them congratulating him on his victory. Ash wanted to believe that Avani was just being hard on him to make him stronger, and more resilient. He would win over the grumpy Guardian if it took him the rest of his life.

As the crowd died down and dispersed, Ash noticed one other guy still standing there looking at him. The dude looked odd to Ash; his hair was blindingly white, his eyebrows too. He was tall and skinny, but he could also tell that the guy was muscular and athletic under his clothes.

"Hey, sorry to bother you," the kid said, "my name's Kane."

He reached his hand out to shake it and Ash obliged. It was the most awkward handshake that he could imagine as if Kane didn't know what he was doing, but it was him who was lost.

Kane chuckled and said, "In Asmaria we shake hands a little differently. Here, like this," he loosened their grips and slid his arm down a few inches. They grasped each other's forearm and gave it one squeeze. "That's a real handshake right there."

"Thanks, nobody thought to mention that to me I guess."

"No worries, we can be a forgetful people sometimes."

There was an awkward silence then, and Ash didn't know how to break it. Kane saved him from figuring it out, "So I wanted to talk to you and see if you'd be interested in some training? I know it's random, but I'm a fairly capable mage myself so I thought I'd offer to give you some tips."

Ash thought the guy sounded a little cocky. There seemed to be some mystique behind his words as well.

"Um, I'll think about it. I have to get going right now, but I'll see you around."

Kane didn't seem offended at all, he just simply said, "Cool, I'll see ya around then."

He turned away and Ash watched him for a few more seconds as Kane pulled three throwing stars from a pouch around his waist. He sucked wind energy into his hand, mixing with the weapons, and flung all three of the stars at a target, they soared through the air with crazy speed and embedded themselves into the target. All three hit dead center, leaving Ash impressed as he walked away.

New Friends

The following day Ash went back to the training field to continue his training. He met Quinn outside very early in the morning; dew soaked the blades of grass and the sun was peaking over the trees, lighting up the sky with streaks of orange and pink. Ash thought to himself how beautiful it was. He was looking forward to the day that all this fighting was over and he was able to just live in peace. He wondered what kind of work he would do here. This place wasn't like the U.S. where capitalism ran everything, although the non-magic folk had to do something to contribute. Ash thought back to the hospital staff, they seemed to be normal enough.

People seemed to care about each other and support one another; he imagined the people here meshed better than anywhere else. Ash was completely lost in thought, oblivious to the conversation Quinn was trying to have with him. He only returned to paying attention once they reached their destination.

There was only one other soul out there on the training field; Ash could see the morning sun bouncing off his brilliant white hair. Ash and Quinn approached him just as he sunk a throwing star dead center on a moving, circular target. He turned after hearing their footsteps and said, "Mornin' guys, what's up?"

"Looking to get some good training in today," Quinn said, "I'm assuming you've been here since before the sun came up?"

"Yep, you know me, I like to get started as early as possible."

Ash didn't realize that the two of them knew each other, but it made sense. He felt a pang of jealousy, nonetheless. With more apprehension than he'd intended, Ash said, "What's with the white hair?"

Ash couldn't tell if it bothered Kane or not, but the boy didn't respond anyway. Quinn quickly changed the subject.

"When Kane and I used to train together he would make me get up super early with him to be the first ones out here. We'd stay until the sun dropped in the sky. That's why we're stronger than the other kids our age."

"Ha, I'm pretty sure we're better than most adults too."

Ash's cheeks got hot with more jealousy; he did not enjoy thinking about the two of them spending so much time alone together. He wondered if this was what it was like to have a crush on someone. There was no other explanation for how he was feeling, but maybe it was just the teenage hormones. He pushed the thoughts aside for the time being, there would be time to figure out how he feels later on.

"Well, let's get to it," Ash said, "we're burning daylight."

The three of them got started right away. Kane led them in a jog around the field to get their bodies warmed up for the day. They started the training session with some hand-to-hand combat. They boxed and grappled like it was a real fight, only holding back their punches so as not to injure each other. Ash felt a little awkward fighting Quinn like this; he'd never fought a girl before and wasn't sure if he should be taking it easy on her or not. That question was answered for him by Kane.

"Come on Newby, stop taking it easy on her, she's kicking your butt!" he shouted after Quinn flung Ash to the ground with a shoulder throw. He picked himself up and brushed the dirt off his clothes, resolving to put forth more effort. She came at him with a flying side kick which he stepped around. He threw a combo of punches at her, one of them landing lightly on her chin. She retaliated, striking back at him with a combo of her own, hitting him with a solid leg kick.

Ash threw a straight jab, but this was a feint; Quinn did what was expected and covered to block the punch but instead blocked her vision, giving him an opening. Ash shot in low on her legs, grabbing the back of them and pressing forward. He took her to the ground and mounted on top of her, pulling his arm back in a position to strike.

Quinn threw her hands up and yelled, "I yield! I yield!".

He climbed off of her and reached his hand out to help her up and she took it. Once standing, she looked into his eyes, lingering long enough to make him blush. Luckily for Ash, Kane came to his rescue from this situation.

"Alright lightning boy, my turn."

Ash chuckled, forgetting about his jealousy of him, "You sure you can handle it?"

Kane just smirked in response. They began their battle, combos were thrown, letting their hands fly freely. It was a wonderful show of skill. Ash would a glimpse of Quinn smiling every so often.

It took a minute for a single blow to be landed, the two boys were both so skilled with fighting that it was difficult for either to strike the other. Finally, Ash landed an elbow to Kane's jaw; he tried to follow it up with a knee, but Kane caught his leg and tripped him. Ash tried to roll over, but Kane saw his opportunity and jumped on his back, putting him in a chokehold. Ash tapped on his arm, signifying that he had given up and the fight was over.

They all bumped fists and took a break. Once they were ready to get back to work, more people began showing up and taking part in their training. Elements flew around in the air, striking targets and each other.

"Okay," Ash asked, "what's next?"

Kane waved for them to follow and led them over to a weapons area. He picked up an assortment of weaponry, from daggers to maces, throwing stars to spears. He tossed them into the air and began juggling them, using wind to keep them aloft and manipulate their direction. After showing off for a minute he began flicking his fingers towards the human-shaped targets. One by one the weapons impaled themselves into the targets with perfect precision.

Quinn and Ash both tried to do the same with just one small dagger; Quinn's landed on the outer edge of the target, but Ash missed completely. Lightning was not great at holding onto inanimate objects. He decided to just stick with the bow and arrow for real battles.

The group of kids ended the training day early and headed back to Kane's house for dinner. House is a poor description of what it appeared to be, which was a mansion. The luxurious home was up a long driveway at the top of a hill; it had a high archway in the front and a large porch that wrapped around the whole house. From the front porch, you could see the entire city in all its glory.

They entered through the tall golden doors and greeted Kane's family. This was the sort of family that Ash had dreamed about. It was obvious to Ash that they were insanely loaded for Asmarian standards, seeing as almost everyone he'd encountered lived in the same comfort. He became curious about what line of work they were in. Kane and his mom showed them around while his dad was reading something in his office. Their house had four bathrooms, six bedrooms, and an indoor pool; Ash couldn't help but wonder why they needed such a large home with just the three of them living there.

Dinner was a feast; rolls, fish, pork, all the meat you could think of! Different kinds of pasta and veggie dishes hit the spot for Ash. They talked and laughed all night, and finished dinner off with an array of pies and cakes. At one point Ash asked what they did for a living and both parents just looked at each other, smiled, and dismissed the question.

"Mrs. Volorium," Ash started, "thank you so much for having us for dinner. This has been such a great night."

"My pleasure dear, any friends of Kane's are always welcome in our home."

Is he my friend? Ash thought to himself. He decided that, yes, they were indeed friends. Hopefully, with time their friendship would grow, but for now, he was sated with how things were. He knew that the days ahead may be grim, but for now, he wanted to make the most of his life.

Frost Mountain

Ash and Kane met up the day after having dinner with Kane's parents; Kane wanted to show him one of the best sights Asmaria had to offer. He was waiting outside of Ash's home when the boy left, jumping out from behind a small bush, startling him. The two headed down the street, laughing jovially.

The sun crept higher into the sky as they walked and talked, entering the forest, and caused the nocturnal creatures to scurry back into their homes. An array of birds were already chirping, filling Ash's head with a morning song.

Ash asked, "Where are we going anyway? You never told me."

"It's called Frost Mountain. The highest point in Asmaria." Kane told him with a large smile.

"Why's it called Frost Mountain? Asmaria is tropical."

Kane snickered, "Just wait til we get there, you'll see. I can tell you've never ventured anywhere, there are plenty of mountains around the world with snow at the top while being surrounded by warm weather."

A look crossed Ash's face that made Kane feel bad. He said, "I'm sorry if that was rude. I didn't mean anything by it."

"It's okay. Don't worry about it."

They didn't make much noise while walking along the steep

trail, and around halfway up, tragedy almost struck Ash. A snake was dangling from a branch; as Ash walked underneath it, unaware of its presence, the snake fell. Inches from landing on Ash's head, Kane turned after hearing it slip on the branch, and quickly blasted it away with wind from his palm.

"Whoa! What the heck was that?" Ash laughed, he wasn't exactly afraid of snakes, but would have been if he'd known what kind of snake that was.

Kane wasn't amused, "That was an Asmarian tree viper; a bite from one of those will leave you dead before you hit the dirt."

Ash's eyes became wide as he said, "Duly noted."

After walking uphill for several miles, Kane finally used the wind to carry the two of them further up the mountain. He lifted them, higher and higher, the air became very chilly as they passed through a cloud. When they popped up through the white fluff, the peak of Frost Mountain was in their view.

The magnificent snow-capped mountains appeared, just as Kane remembered them. He laded the two of them on a nearby ledge as gingerly as he could but Ash still tumbled to the ground. Kane chuckled as he helped him back to his feet.

There was a nest a few meters away, with two large white birds with long necks and short black beaks. The creatures squawked at them as they slowly approached.

Ash looked worried as he asked, "Are you sure it's okay to get so close?"

"Oh yeah, these guys are pretty docile. They're just saying hello. These are the babies anyway."

A look of shock crossed Ash's face. He asked, "These things are already half my size. How big are the parents?"

His question was answered when a shadow covered him and

the massive bird called out from above.

He spun around, standing in the shadow of this amazing bird, who eyed him warily. Kane walked straight up to it, passing Ash, and setting the beast at ease. The imposing bird towered over him and relaxed upon recognizing an old friend. It craned its lengthy neck down, to which Kane stroked gently, and then waved Ash forward.

Ash approached, the snow crunching beneath his feet, and came to the other side of the bird. He tentatively placed a hand on its neck as well, "So, what are they called?"

"The brodagian crane. They can only live up here, this high in the mountain tops. Their imposing size leaves them with no predators, other than large cats, which we do have in the jungle. They're friendly creatures though, and choose to live up here where the cats can't reach them. They venture down the mountain in the day to collect food for themselves and their babies."

Kane reached down, grabbing a tuft of feathers on the bird's chest, pulling it back to reveal a rather large pouch. Inside was an assortment of fruits the mother bird had plucked and foraged for down in the trees.

Kane sneakily retreated away from Ash as he stroked the crane's neck. He went behind a huge rock and bent down, scooping up a handful of snow as he did. He shaped it into a sphere and then packed the snow in as tightly as he could. Once the perfect snowball was formed he whirled it at Ash.

Whap!

The snowball smacked Ash in the back of his head and burst. Ash whirled around, looking ready for a fight. *He must have never been in a snowball fight before*, Kane thought. Kane grinned at him from behind his cover. Ash just stood there, staring at him. Kane had already formed another snowball and flung this one at him as well.

Ash tried to catch it, but the snowball exploded in his palm and the powder spattered his face. Kane threw his head back, laughing heartily. Ash finally caught on to the game and bent down to gather his own snowball.

Kane vacated his hiding spot and the two boys spent a long time flinging the balls of snow at each other. They were both sweating from the exertion by the time the mighty battle had concluded. They plopped down on a stump, breathing hard together.

The bitter wind and the sweat caused them both to shiver in the cold weather. Kane asked Ash if he was ready to head back down the mountain and he told him that he was.

"Hold on tight," he said as he grabbed Ash's hand and leaped from the edge of the cliff. They dove down through the sky, plummeting toward the trees. Kane caught them with a couple hundred feet to go and slowly lowered them to the ground, where they stood for a moment to soak up the warmth.

"I think I'd just fly everywhere if I could control the wind. I haven't quite figured out how to propel myself through the air with lightning, and I'm pretty sure it's impossible," Ash stated.

"Trust me, it gets very tiring, very quickly. There's a reason why I don't travel all over the place through the air."

They made their way back towards the city after resting for a moment and discussed what their plans were for the following day. Ash told him that Quinn was supposed to show him around the city some more, and maybe the Great Tree. Kane made some jokes about the two of them dating, but Ash looked embarrassed. Kane took note of this and let it go, and instead told him how cool Quinn was.

Walking back through the jungle gave them enough time to get to know each other a bit more. Ash told Kane about his life in New York which led him to understand why the kid had never been in a snowball fight or anything. He thought how sad it was that he had never been able to see anything but the few walls inside their home until now.

Ash asked Kane, "So, I've been wondering something. After seeing your house and how massive it is, what is it that your parents do for a living?"

Kane took a moment, wondering how much he should tell. He decided on the truth. "My family comes from a long line of water mages. For a long time, they've been charged with protecting the island from outsiders. You've learned that Asmaria has been kept secret from the rest of the world for the most part. That's because we have teams of water mages constantly posted around the island to control the seas surrounding us. The majority of these water users come from my family.

"Because it's such an important job, we are given whatever lifestyle we wish. So, my parents choose to live in a mansion that is far too big. But it does make for a great party though."

Ash nodded his head, "Well, they seem cool enough anyway. I'd live in a mansion if I got a choice."

The sun was setting when they finally made it back to the Capitol, and they split off to go back to their houses, saying goodbye. Kane made it back to his too-big of a home and went to his room. His footsteps echoing in its empty halls. He loved his parents but sometimes wished that they were around more. This house was far too large for him to be alone in it all the time.

The Great Tree

The next day, after a great night of sleep for Ash, Quinn showed him more of the city, where he could get food for his house and then his new mage outfit. It had to be specially made because there were no purple outfits in stock for obvious reasons. It was very soft, but Ash felt like he stuck out like a sore thumb, since no one else had on purple.

They made their way towards the center of the island so Quinn could show him the Great Tree. He asked, "Can you tell me more about this tree? I don't get how everything here could come from it."

"I know it's kind of hard to understand, but you'll get it when you see it. According to all of our history books the Great Tree has been around for as long as we have. No one knows the origin of the Tree though. The Tree is where all of our powers come from, and we're not sure how it works, but when you're there you can feel the immense presence of power and life. It's as if the Tree is a deity that gives life to all of Asmaria. The Great Tree is sacred, which is why we bury our people there. It has given us such life that we must do all we can to keep it healthy and thriving. It may sound brutal, but our bodies provide all the nutrients the Tree needs."

"Wow. It sounds a bit weird, but I still can't wait to see it.

Maybe then it'll make more sense to me."

They made their way out of the city and down a beaten path amongst the trees and flowers. Along the way, Ash spotted all sorts of creatures he'd never seen before. There were birds of every color, lizards that could walk on their hind legs, and he even saw what resembled a groundhog with the tail of an opossum and the claws of a sloth. That one freaked him out a bit. There were giant insects, butterflies the size of his face, and spiders that moved with such speed they could have been tiny cheetahs. Quinn assured him that he would be okay, as long as he stayed on the paths the animals and insects here wouldn't bother him.

They approached a wide, natural river where they hopped across protruding stones to get to the other side. In the river, Ash saw a fish with eyes that bulged from its skull and had sharp, jagged teeth. He also spotted a green frog with orange spots all over its back. After crossing the river they climbed a tall hill and on the other side was the Great Tree.

Ash had never seen anything like it before. The tree was massive, bigger than the California Redwoods that he'd seen on TV. The tree was alive with color; there were five colors that he noticed, orange, green, blue, white, and purple. The tree glowed as the colors swirled around its trunk.

"I don't even know what to say. This is the most beautiful thing I've ever laid eyes on," he said.

"Yeah, you're right about that. We have a ritual that we do every time we visit the Tree. It's going to sound weird, but you'll understand why after we do it."

There was a small stone table near the base of the Tree with a blade on it. The blade had intricate designs on the handle and was about eight inches long in total. Ash watched as Quinn walked over to the the table, picked up the knife, and cut her palm open dripping some of her blood onto the exposed roots. The vibrant colors on the tree pulsated.

Ash gasped and rushed to her side but she said, "No, wait. This is all part of it. Just wait, you're next." He backed off and watched her.

After dripping a few drops of her blood she walked over to a low-hanging branch and held her hand up to it, whispering, with barely enough volume for Ash to hear, "Thank you for all that you do." The branch wrapped around her hand of its own volition and after a few seconds, it let go, leaving her hand healed from the self-inflicted wound.

"Okay, now it's your turn," Quinn said after wiping off the blade and placing it back down on the stone table. Not wanting to do it, but gathering up the courage to do so, Ash walked over to the table and did as she had done.

He picked up the blade and placing the sharp edge on his palm, he dragged it across quickly. It stung and he winced but continued. His blood dripped down on the roots and the tree seemed to shudder. He walked over to the branch and whispered, "Thank you for all that you do." And just as before the branch wrapped itself around his hand. Ash then felt a connection to the Great Tree. It was as if the thing was alive and speaking to him through his mind.

Once the branch released him he stepped back and turned to face Quinn who had a big smile on her face. "So, what do you think? Not so bad huh?"

"It's like, the Tree was telling me that everything would be okay. That I would be strong enough to accomplish anything that I set my mind to. Thank you for bringing me here. This was a great experience."

Quinn said, "You're welcome. I'm glad I was the one who got to bring you here."

They made their way back toward their homes where Quinn gave Ash some books to study up on the history of Asmaria. Most teenage boys probably would have just blown it off, but Ash doesn't mind reading. History was always entertaining for him anyway.

He entered his humble abode and started making some dinner from the groceries he had just gotten. Luckily he often had to make his food because Rick would be at work, so he's no stranger to cooking. Tonight had spaghetti on the menu. From being at Quinn's, Charlie's, and his own home he noticed that no one had a TV, which made sense as most other things around here weren't what he was used to. He began reading the books that he'd gotten and came upon an article that talked about the outlawing of television. There is no crime in Asmaria, apart from isolated attacks from the Forbidden, but the punishment for crime of any sort was devastating.

After being forced to banish several young adults from the island a hundred years ago, the Guardians agreed everyone would benefit if they all lived differently from the rest of the world. The citizens were forced to comply or be banished for breaking the law. Most forms of technology were abandoned along with television.

Upon reading about past violence within the Asmarian people he came across something rather interesting. There wasn't a whole lot of information about the Forbidden, but he did read that they draw their power from something similar to the Great Tree. They're not sure exactly what it is or where it's even located, but they know if exists. Roughly two hundred years ago there was a war between the Asmarians and the

Forbidden. Thousands of the dark-cloaked villains stormed the Northern beach of Asmaria where the Guild—who were outnumbered—converged to defend their home. A deadly battle ensued but the Guild came out on top, pushing enemy forces back and taking a few prisoners back with them.

The prisoners of the Northern beach battle were brought back to the city and interrogated by the Guardians of that time. This is how they learned that the Forbidden worship an evil demon who goes by the name of Aros. The demon has some sort of object that gives these people power over darkness. They also learned that the Forbidden are all Asmarians who were born without power, which explains why they would partner up with a demon for the ability to control darkness.

Moving onto different books, there was one about the Great Tree where Ash was able to see more about the burial ritual. The person is placed at the base of the tree on the ground. A prayer of thanks is said by one individual and then the crowd repeats it. After that the roots of the tree claw themselves out from under the dirt and wrap the deceased person up, dragging them down into the soil where they will be dissolved, sending their life force back into the Tree.

After reading about the burial ritual, he thought of his mother and wondered if her spirit was out there somewhere, watching him. A single tear streaked down his face and dripped from his chin. He wiped it away fervently, trying to be the strong boy that he thought she'd want him to be.

All he wanted at that moment was to be wrapped in her arms, with her telling him everything would be okay. He decided he had read enough for the night. He closed the book, tossed it on the kitchen counter, and wandered to his bed where he flopped down and quickly fell asleep.

Preparing For War

Over the next week, Ash would train every day to face the master of the Forbidden. He trained long, hard days, practicing his lightning control more than anything. He excelled at hand-to-hand combat, using his experience boxing Rick as a baseline. He was even able to teach a thing or two about boxing to some of the other kids; the adults were less forthcoming about wanting help from someone much younger than them. The grappling arts were more difficult for him. It was very foreign, but eventually, he was able to hold his own against the other kids his size.

He often thought about his father who was being held captive. He would ponder if this was even worth it. He never knew his father and didn't know if they would even get along. Each time these thoughts pressed into his mind he would just remind himself that it didn't matter. The right thing to do would be to do his best to save him from the clutches of Ozul. Even if it was a random person, he would still try his best to save them.

Ash saw Kane almost every day, and they would often train together. Kane was a great teacher when it came to controlling abilities, but he would regularly disappear without a trace and Ash never knew where the boy ran off to. Ash meandered about at times, wondering if Kane and Quinn were together somewhere, the ugly head of jealousy daring to show itself yet again.

On the last day of the next week, he met another kid who was a couple of years older. His name was Juda. The two met during a sparring session where everything except magic was allowed. Juda was a bit bigger than Ash, he was a few inches taller and weighed at least 20 more pounds. In the end, Juda was the victor, after he kicked Ash hard enough in the stomach to send him spiraling into the dirt.

After training was finished, Juda helped Ash up and brushed him off, giving him a high five. "Ya know, there's not many here who can keep me on my toes like that," Juda said, giving Ash a small boost of pride.

"Thanks. I appreciate you taking the time out of your day to work with me. I feel like I'm leagues behind everyone else here."

"No worries. We all have to be ready for what's to come. For a while now I thought the Forbidden had slithered into their holes and died, but I guess that's not true. Tomorrow we should work on some weapons training."

"I'm down for that. I've struggled in that area as well, it's all very different from what I'm used to."

Laughing Juda said, "Don't worry about it. No one is good at everything, and if they are, you can bet they put in a ton of hours to reach that point. Just by looking at you, I'd say you're good with a spear, based on how short you are."

Ash didn't like being called short by this guy, seeing as they'd only just met, but he let it go.

Juda gulped down a whole canteen of water and then asked, "Hey, you wanna go hang out for a bit?"

"Sure, I've got no one to go home to right?"

"That makes two of us," Juda said with a laugh.

They made their way through the street and down to Juda's home. His house was nowhere near any others which was weird to Ash. Inside was very dull with nothing on the walls, cracked paint, and dusty counters. It gave Ash an unsettled feeling in his stomach.

"So," Juda, trying to start the conversation, "how are you liking Asmaria so far?"

"Oh, it's been great. I never got to meet my real dad, but he's been held captive by the Forbidden this whole time. Rick, my adoptive father, never let me leave our apartment. I know he was just trying to protect me, but it made me resent him a little, I couldn't wait to get out of there, but I also hurt him pretty bad and I feel awful about it. What about you? Why do you live alone?"

Ash noticed Juda's expression darken as he said, "I grew up rough. My mother ditched us shortly after I was born. My father beat me for the smallest things. Told me I was a waste of time. I'm just now finding the strength to prove him wrong and make a legacy for myself."

"Okay, but is he still alive? Is he here?"

"No. He's very, very far away. Listen, don't tell anyone about this conversation okay? My dad was a powerless mage who turned to the Forbidden. I don't want anyone asking questions about it."

"I won't say anything. I'm sorry that you had to grow up like that."

They spent a while in conversation about training and such and then Ash decided it was time he went back to his own house.

Ash left Juda's home and walked back to his own where he

promptly crashed on the bed without any dinner, his body wrought with exhaustion. That night he had restless sleep; every time he would fall asleep he found himself in a recurring nightmare. He was standing before the shadowy silhouettes of the Forbidden leader and his father who was still gagged and bound. He tried producing lightning to fire at the dark lord, but nothing would happen. It ended the same each time, with Ash being suffocated by dark tendrils while the evil man laughed maniacally.

The next day Ash met up with Juda on the training field. He was already getting the weapons prepared before Ash arrived. He noticed Ash walking up and said, "Hey man, you ready for a fun-filled day of fighting?"

"Yeah, I'm as ready as I'll ever be."

"You sound kinda down. Everything okay?"

"Yeah, I just couldn't sleep last night. Kept having the same nightmare that I couldn't produce lightning and got choked out by the shadows."

"Sheesh. That's rough. Let's take your mind off it."

Ash wasn't for sure, but he thought he saw Juda smirk as he turned away from him.

They began training, first taking things slow. They needed to figure out what Ash was good at, there were only 20 days left until the deadline so they would find out Ash's strength and then build on that. Learning different weapons would have to come later. With a short sword, Ash was halfway decent. He couldn't beat Juda, but he did last longer than he expected to. Next came the spear which was too heavy for him to do anything with. Lastly was the bow and arrow. He found a short bow that was light and not too difficult for him to pull back.

Ash enjoyed the bow and was able to hit close to the center

of the targets almost every time. Juda would throw wooden discs into the air to simulate a moving target which made it much harder to hit. It took a few tries before he was able to nail one, but after he found his rhythm it was easy for him. He took the bow home with him that night to practice drawing it back, working the shakiness out of his arms, and then slept peacefully until morning came.

The Boy Unknown

After training so vigorously over the previous week Ash decided to take a day off to do some more exploring. He found Quinn and convinced her to show him something cool. She told him that there was a beautiful beach where they could spend the day relaxing. They made the journey to the North shore of the island, the very same one from the history book Ash had read, although now there was no sign of battle there. It didn't take them too long to arrive despite it being the furthest distance he'd traveled on the island so far. Quinn created a wave of water that carried them quickly across the island and to the beach. Once there, they walked barefooted through the sand while Ash admired the breathtaking beauty before them.

Baby blue seagulls were passing by overhead, almost blending in with the sky above them. Ash marveled at the wondrous scene around them, wanting this moment to last forever. He always wanted to visit a beach, but this was better than any experience he could have imagined.

The beach was covered in tiny pebbles that seemed to glow a bright blue even in the daylight. Ash could only imagine how brightly it would glow at night time. There were various sizes of shells all over the place, but most important to Ash, Quinn looked magnificent with the sea breeze blowing through her hair. The beach was pristine, the water crystal clear; Ash hated knowing that he would eventually have to leave this gorgeous spot.

"I've never seen a beach before. It's so beautiful here, I never want to leave."

"Well, I don't blame you there. I've been meaning to ask you, how has training been going? I've been so busy running errands that I haven't been able to make it down to the field to visit you."

"It's going pretty well. I met this guy named Juda; he and I have been training like crazy. Sparring is fun, but I don't think he has any magic, or maybe I just haven't seen him use any."

Quinn had a puzzled look on her face as she said, "Juda? I've never heard of him."

"Well, ya know it is a big island after all. I doubt you know everyone."

"Look, Asmaria isn't all that massive and I've met pretty much everyone that trains at the field at least once. If you're training to become a warrior of the Guild then I would know. Trust me, there's something off about this guy."

"Okay. I'll just have to be careful. When we get back I'll ask Kane about him. For now, I'd like to just enjoy the beach."

Quinn reluctantly agreed to relax for a bit, as they waded in the pellucid water and admired the unique assortment of fish that swam by. Ash spotted some sort of crab that was the size of a small dog, but it had six eyes instead of two, and he made a mental note to steer clear of that thing and watch where he stepped.

After a couple of hours in the warm sun, Ash was beginning to feel crisp. His skin wasn't used to being outside at all. He told

Quinn that he was ready to head back and get some training in, but he just wanted to go talk to Kane about Juda. It was unsettling that Quinn was so certain she'd never heard of him.

Once they made it back into the city Ash headed straight to the training field where he knew Kane would be. He entered the grounds, looking around to spot his friend. He also kept an eye out for Juda, just in case the boy was around. He didn't see him anywhere though. He saw Kane's brilliant white hair shining in the afternoon sun.

Ash jogged over to Kane as he worked on lifting large stones with his wind magic.

"Hey Kane. Whatcha up to?"

Kane sat a large boulder down heavily and said, "Just working on my endurance with lifting heavy objects." He was breathing laboriously.

"Sorry to interrupt but there was something I wanted to talk to you about."

"Don't worry about it. What's on your mind? Trying to figure out how I became so cool?" he said with a chuckle.

Ash laughed, "Whoever told you that you were cool?"

Kane jumped on Ash and the two boys wrestled playfully until Ash was able to break away from his grasp. They both laughed happily.

Ash said, "Really though, I have a question about someone I met."

"Oh? A girl?" Kane said with a sly grin."

"Nah, his name is Juda. I met him out here the other day. We trained together for a bit and then I went back to his place to hang out. His house seemed like no one had been living there. It was all rundown and dusty. And when I mentioned it to Quinn, she said she'd never heard of him before. There's no way you guys know everyone here right?"

Kane stood with crossed arms and then rested his chin on one of his hands while Ash spoke. When he awaited an answer, Kane said, "Well, Quinn and I are very different people. I tend to keep to myself and she is more outgoing and social. It would make more sense if it was just me who had never heard of this Juda. It's true, I've never met anyone by that name. It concerns me more that Quinn doesn't know of him though. I think we should check out his place."

Ash crept around a tree just outside of the shack that he remembered to be Juda's home. Kane peered around from behind a different tree. They watched it silently for several minutes and when no one came or went, Kane motioned for Ash to follow him.

They ran up to the house in a crouch, trying to be as quiet as possible. When they reached the house, the boys leaned up against it and listened for any noise coming from inside. Kane peeked over a window frame into the house and then stood up straight.

He said, "I don't see anyone in there. Let's go check it out."

Ash walked to the front door and tried the nob. It was unlocked. He shoved it open, waiting to enter just in case. The inside was dark and Ash didn't hear any sounds coming from within. Mustering courage, he stepped inside and Kane followed.

"It looks like no one has been living here," Kane said.

Ash looked around more carefully than he had the first time. There were cobwebs in every corner of the room. Every surface was covered in a thick layer of dust except for the spots where they had sat before.

"I can't believe I didn't notice how off this was before," Ash said, shaking his head.

Kane placed a hand on his shoulder, "Don't be so hard on yourself. It could have happened to anyone."

"I guess my need for friendship clouded my judgment."

Kane didn't respond and continued to look around. Ash silently cursed himself for being so vulnerable in front of him.

"One thing's for sure; Juda isn't who he says he is. We need to keep a close eye on him. Next time you see him, come find me."

"What, you think I can't handle him on my own?" Ash asked with indignation.

Kane shook his head, "That's not it. I just want to help."

Ash walked out of the house and headed back to his own. Kane trailed behind him and they didn't speak. Ash was trying to out-pace him without letting him notice. He felt that Kane believed he wasn't capable of handling himself.

Once back at his home, he developed a plan of action for Juda. He was going to get to the bottom of this by himself and prove to Kane that he didn't need his help with everything. All he had to do was find Juda and then get some answers out of him. How hard could it be?

A Secret Revealed

I t was getting dark, the sun was almost completely hidden beneath the horizon. Ash scoured all the places he'd been to so far, looking around for Juda. He finally found him exiting the jungle on the path that leads to the Great Tree. Ash didn't think he looked particularly suspicious right now. He blended in just as everyone else did.

He followed him back to his house. Ash waited a moment before approaching and then slid up to the side. As he approached he heard a yell come from inside. He couldn't make out what it said or who it was, but they were indeed angry about something. He cupped his hands around an ear and held them up against the door.

Ash heard two voices inside the house. One of them was Juda, and the other sounded familiar but he couldn't quite place it. The voice was a deep growl, as if it didn't belong to someone quite human, but rather a beast. It sounded like the stranger was berating Juda for something. What he heard Juda say next was rather disturbing and left Ash with wobbly legs and clammy hands.

"I want to kill him, Father, please! Let me just end this now, he's so weak!"

Ash was trying to process what was happening and then the

voice responded, "No! How many times must I tell you, he is mine to take care of? Your task is to observe and report back to me. Now, tell me, what have you learned?"

Ash moved around to a side window and found a small crack that he could peep through. There was a large rock that he tip-toed on to get a better look inside. He was able to see Juda sitting on his couch in front of the fireplace. In the fireplace, orange flames flickered about, but coming from the flames was the masked shadowy face of the same man who presented himself as the leader of the Forbidden. Ash gasped and fell backward off the rock, making enough noise to alert the two inside the ramshackle hut.

Fear coursed through his veins as Ash jumped up and began running away from Juda's house, but it was too late. In the time that it had taken for Ash to recover from falling over, Juda was able to get out the door and jump in front of him. He stood in the way of Ash with his arms crossed and a wide, cunning smile on his face that made him look like a psycho. His eyes were wild.

Juda, with a nasty smile on his face, said, "So, how much did you hear?"

Ash attempted to sound tough by putting as much venom into his words as possible, "I heard enough, traitor. Just one question, who are you?"

"Oh, I didn't lie about who I am. Not totally anyway. My name really is Juda, and my father is one of the Forbidden. But I am not here as one of the Asmarian warriors. Come back with me Ash. With the Forbidden, you would gain so much power, and you could be reunited with your father!"

The temptation to join Juda was real for Ash as he yearned for his father. He would have even settled for Rick at this point.

Juda could see the dilemma going through Ash's mind and thought he had won him over.

He held out his hand to Ash and said, "Join me, Ash. You know you want to. You have unrivaled potential, I've seen it! Just take my hand, and you can be with your real family forever."

Ash looked up at him and with determination said, "No!" Smacking his hand away, Ash sprung into action. He shot up from the dirt, blasting a straight right punch targeting Juda's nose. At the last possible second Juda spun away, effortlessly dodging the punch and delivering a swift knee to Ash's stomach.

Ash doubled over as Juda laughed and said, "You are no match for me. You should have joined me when you had the chance. You're just lucky I'm not allowed to kill you. Although, Dad never said I couldn't have fun with you."

Juda lunged at Ash trying to grab his wrist, but he had recovered in time to evade the hold. Remembering his training with lightning, Ash let the power course through him, from his mind down to his hands, faster this time, without having to close his eyes. He thrust his hands toward his enemy and let the power go, shooting a narrow beam of purple lightning toward Juda. Before the lightning was able to reach its target, Juda brought his arms up into an X formation, manipulating the darkness around them to form a shield that the lightning could not penetrate.

As Ash released the blast and tried to evaluate what just happened, Juda swiftly moved next to him with incredible speed. He hit Ash clean across the jaw with a left hook and then a kick to the sternum. Ash tried swinging back but was dizzy from the strike to his face, he swung wildly. It was as if he had never boxed a day in his life before. Perhaps he should have gotten more practice with absorbing blows to his face. Juda easily dodged or blocked each pathetic attempt of a strike from Ash who was becoming more and more drained of energy.

He tried to summon more lightning but the only thing that would appear was small, purple, sputtering sparks. His body was riddled with bruises, and his head felt like mush. Blood leaked from his lips.

Juda grabbed Ash by his wrist and dragged him into a choke hold from behind. He kicked Ash in the bend of his knee knocking him to the ground. Juda walked around in front of him and gathered up balls of darkness in his palm. He wiggled his fingers which turned the harmless-looking spheres of black into five, three-inch-long shards of death. He gave Ash a swift kick to his nose which exploded with blood gushing down his face as he fell onto his back. He used his free hand to create a tendril of shadow that held one of his arms to the ground and then shot a single black shard into it, pinning it to the Earth.

One by one, Juda would use an arm of darkness to hold down Ash's limbs just to fling a spike into them. With each body part that was nailed down, the pain lessened. Eventually, Ash stopped screaming altogether. Juda stood over him, looking triumphant.

He said, "You shouldn't have been so stubborn kid. Do you *really* think you're going to take on Lord Ozul? You can't even defeat me. I mean, I know I'm pretty awesome, but still, you're in way over your head. Should have just come back quietly with me."

With that final sentence, Juda whistled and a black horse with wings appeared from the shadows. He didn't have the energy to attempt screaming for help. Ash thought this was the end for him and part of him was ready for it to be over. There was no way he could move, and no one was going to find him. Giving into his pain he let the fatigue and pain take over him. He slipped into darkness, hoping that he wouldn't wake up.

Epiphany

Ash once again woke up in the hospital with the sound of beeps and the smell of rubbing alcohol. His vision was blurry as his eyes fluttered open and he tried to make sense of his surroundings. Once his eyes focused he saw that he was wearing a lot of bandages. His nose throbbed and looked to be recently mended. There was a tube down his throat, causing him to choke a little, so he decided to pull it out on his own which sent one of the machines next to him into a frenzy.

A nurse ran in and said, "Goodness, what do you think you're doing?" She helped him pull the tube the rest of the way out and gave him some water to drink, shaking her head and mumbling as she left.

A few minutes later in walked Quinn and Brandr. "Hey, how ya feeling?" Quinn asked with tears in her eyes.

Ash's throat was raw and his voice was raspy, "I'm okay I guess. I can't believe I was so stupid."

Brandr had been staring at the floor but looked up once it became quiet and said, "Ash, I'm so sorry this happened to you. It's all our fault, we failed you. We should have been more attentive to your training process. Had we noticed this impostor sooner, none of it would have happened. I still don't understand how he was able to infiltrate us."

"It's okay. I don't blame any of you. I should have been stronger. If I was ready then Juda would be the one in here right now."

Ash sounded defeated, but somewhere inside him, a fiery rage burned, forcing him to think about getting back out there to train. He tried sitting up more but his body ached so badly that he winced.

Quinn rushed forward to help him up, smiling as he looked up into her blue eyes. "Don't worry. I'm not leaving your side again. I'm going to make sure nothing like this happens to you from here on."

Brandr told Ash that he had been in a coma for about a week now, leaving only fifteen days before he was supposed to meet with Ozul at Birkwood Park. After that, Brandr asked him to explain everything that had happened. He went through the entire story, about how they first started training together. He told him about the rundown house that Juda was living in and how he told him just enough about his past to get Ash to trust him. He told him about Quinn's distrust and that he didn't take it seriously until he and Kane checked the place out together.

As he recounted the night that he was almost murdered, Brandr focused on his story, listening intently and not saying a single word. The focus behind his orange eyes was so intense that Ash almost wanted to recede further into the bed. He told them every little detail about their fight and how his moves were useless against him.

After he was done telling the whole story Brandr said, "I promise we will get you up to speed. I vow to make you the greatest warrior Asmaria has ever seen."

Ash smiled, chuckling softly, "Just make sure you don't get

jealous when I become more skilled than you."

Brandr made the room shake with his booming laughter and Quinn just giggled. He said, "I'll be seeing you on the training field in three days. The nursing staff believes with their special healing remedies that you'll be back on your feet within that time. We don't have much of that to waste so training will begin as soon as you can."

"Got it. I'll see you then."

After Brandr left the room Quinn said, "I was very worried about you, like, more worried than I've ever been about someone."

At this moment Ash became aware that Quinn *actually* cared about him. He never imagined that he could feel this close to another person.

He took her hand in his and smiled, unable to form the words he wanted to express. She looked more beautiful to him than ever now and he was worried he'd never work up the courage to tell her how much he liked her. After this, he wasn't sure that he'd survive the next battle. No matter what it takes, he must become stronger. He must be the best version of himself, if not for anyone else, then for Quinn.

Quinn and Ash spent the rest of the day together in that hospital room just talking about themselves and their past. Ash learned that she was the only mage in her family. There hasn't been one for as long as any of them can remember, but they were all so happy when she was the one who broke the family curse, as they called it. He learned that she was just a few months older than him.

They were enjoying each other's company when in walked his new friend, Kane. He had a big dumb smile on his face. Ash grinned back at him, happy to see him despite feeling embarrassed.

"What's up, old man?" Ash teased.

"Oh yeah, back with the hair jokes, huh?"

He sat at the foot of Ash's bed, speaking about his day. He looked glum when Ash recounted everything he'd been through. When he was finished with his tale, Kane was back on his feet, pacing the room. A gentle breeze seemed to flow around him, causing nearby papers to fly about. He stared at his feet for a moment until he turned his face back to Ash.

"I should have been there. I would have torn that kid to shreds!"

"It's okay. It's my fault. I thought I could take him alone. I shouldn't have been so careless."

"Yeah. We'll get him back though. I'll make sure of that."

Kane was finally able to calm down, and he and Quinn said their goodbyes to each other, leaving just Quinn and Ash once again. She tousled his hair for a moment before planting a kiss on his forehead, and saying goodbye. His stomach hummed with butterflies as she walked away, and all he wanted was to go with her.

Quinn left the hospital but was back in the morning before Ash had even woken up himself. It was refreshing to see her first thing in the morning, and in the next couple of days, it was a routine for them. They'd spend all day getting to know each other better and then repeat the next day. When Ash was cleared by the infirmary to return to training he walked out with Quinn, a spring in his step. He was excited to get back on the horse and truly grow into the warrior he knew he could be.

They started the first day of training with Brandr and Charlie. They were working on getting the mind-to-body connection faster so that he could wield his lightning more efficiently. After hours of sweating it clicked in his brain, a wondrous epiphany that woke him up and left him activating his powers in a split second. He was able to produce his lightning even quicker than old man Charlie. The lightning was now more than just a power that he drew on, it was part of him, an extension of his being.

With ten days left before he was supposed to meet up with Ozul, it was time to grind out the rest of his weaknesses. He needed to turn his body into a machine, so he started getting up early to run and do push-ups, determined to outwork even the hardest worker he knew, Kane. He would use his lunch breaks from training to eat a quick bite and do pull-ups and squats. With the special medicines and foods around Asmaria, Ash's body developed rapidly, his muscle definition had doubled since he arrived on the island. His performance had increased as well; before this point, he struggled to run two laps around the training field, but now he was running twelve at once with hardly any problem.

Brandr told Ash that he and the other Guardians held a Guild meeting and let them all in on the plan to train Ash up in time for the meeting with Ozul. Every day he would spar with 30 different people. They would hone their skills in hand-to-hand combat, beating each other mercilessly, and then eating some heala to fix up their cuts and bruises more quickly. When his rounds were over he would practice smiting targets with his deadly bolts. After the first day back to training, Ash stopped losing rounds, unless it was against Kane of course. Together they were becoming a formidable team, no one would stand in their way. The only issue was the bigger stronger kids and adults. His body had become stronger, but it wasn't quite at the level it needed to be.

Avani

Avani grew up different from most Asmarians. He was 34 years old and had become the youngest Guardian in history at the age of 22. Most Guardians were at least 30 before they stepped into the role of leading the Guild. He had a dark past that forged the grumbling man he is. He often thought about what his life would be like had he not lived through such tragedy.

Avani had quickly moved into the spotlight and outshone his peers. He was becoming a master of his craft and was the beacon of light for his family. His parents held no magical ability.

Avani's parents were proud of him, but they were ashamed to be of no magic, and living in their own son's shadow became too much for them to handle. One night while mostly everyone was in their homes, the couple used the cover of darkness to sneak away and set fire to the Great Tree. Their goal was to burn the tree to ashes thus destroying magic and leaving everyone powerless.

Avani had overheard them discussing the plot and he foiled their plans. He signaled for help and followed them, careful not to be spotted by them. Avani caught them in the act, trying to burn down the Great Tree, and decided to take matters into his own hands. Using his ability, he encapsulated both of them in rock, then forced it to sink deep into the Earth despite listening to their screams. The Guardians arrived just as their heads sank below the ground.

Avani, even so young, understood why they had to be stopped, but there was always a part of him that resented Asmaria itself. Most Asmarians tried to make non-mages feel important, but they often felt inadequate anyway. There was a part of him that also resented and hated himself for choosing to act as their executioner. He used to think that had he not been such a star, maybe they wouldn't have felt the need to do what they'd done. He tried to let it go but the anger and bitterness constantly ate at him. Most of Asmaria had long forgotten what happened to his parents, even his colleagues, but he would never forget.

Avani hoped that one day he would be able to let it go, but today was not that day, and now he had to go help train the new kid.

He didn't trust Ash and could sense a darkness in him, similar to the one that he felt in himself. There was just something off. Other people seemed to trust him and if Avani had to be the one person keeping the boy in check, so be it.

Avani left the Guild building after meeting with the other Guardians; they made small talk as they walked down the street toward the training field. Avani specialized in two things, earth magic and sword fighting. He heard that Ash was particularly gifted with a bow and arrow for someone who never picked one up before. He would put that rumor to the test. Avani hadn't lost a sword fight in such a long time that he couldn't remember who it was that bested him. When they came out to the field it was very early in the morning but Ash was already there practicing his magic on the training targets. Quinn watched from under a nearby tree; she did not stir at the sight of the two men.

As they approached, Brandr said, "Ash, you remember Avani. He's going to be showing you a few things regarding weapons training. I must go attend to some personal business, but I will be back at the end of the day to see how things are going. Don't take it too easy on him. And Avani, play nice." He said the last statement pointedly, making eye contact with Avani.

"So," Ash said, "What should we do first?"

Avani glared at him but said nothing. He walked over to one of the sword stands and grabbed one, tossing it with a spin slightly in the air and slicing it diagonally in front of him in the pattern of an X.

With a yell, "Hyah!" Avani lunged at Ash with the tip of his sword, causing him to yelp and jump out of the way. The sword's tip was just an inch away from piercing the boy in his chest.

"What are you, crazy?" Ash shouted.

"Shut up and fight back. I wanna see what you're made of."

Avani tried for a stab again, this time being parried by the handle of Ash's bow who then retaliated with an attack of his own. The two clashed, sword against the bow, again and again, neither one making any sort of progress. Avani decided to take it up a notch. He gave the ground a stomp with one foot, causing the dirt under Ash to shift around. Ash was focused on keeping his footing on the unstable ground giving Avani his opportunity for attack. He charged slashing his blade, slicing Ash on both arms near his biceps. The cuts weren't deep enough to do any real damage, but it showed who now had the upper hand.

Ash shouted, "What the heck, man? I thought we weren't

using our powers!"

Avani laughed and said, "I never agreed to such terms. Do you think any of your enemies are going to wait for you to be ready to hit you with their abilities? No, so why would I? My job is to prepare you for everything and that's what I'm doing. If you can't handle it, then maybe you should go back to where you came from."

Ash jumped and rolled off the patch of writhing earth, popping up to his feet and summoning the power within him. He shot a bolt of purple lightning at Avani who just barely sidestepped it. Avani then used the ground beneath himself to propel him up into the air and fly towards Ash. He came down with his sword in both hands, the tip pointing down, stabbing the earth as Ash narrowly got out of the way.

Ash began shooting small balls of lightning at Avani who pursued, blocking the little spheres with his sword the whole time. He got within striking range of Ash and feigned going left and went right instead. He twisted Ash's bow up with his sword, disarming him and smacking him on the head with the hilt of his sword. Ash fell to the ground.

Avani, knowing that he was victorious stabbed his sword into the ground and then pointed his hands toward Ash, spread his fingers, and then closed them into fists. The soil around Ash loosened, surrounded him, and then solidified.

Avani picked up his sword, walked over to Ash, put the tip of the blade to his throat, and said, "You lose, you die."

Ash retorted, "But haven't lost."

Ash grinned. Lightning shot up from under his feet just barely missing Avani, and even burning off some of his arm hair in the process. Ash sent lightning throughout his body to break apart the hard dirt and then jumped up. He forced the arcs out of fists and forged them into the shape of swords. Ash charged at Avani this time dodging the dirt and rocks that the earth mage was flinging at him.

Ash closed the distance between them, swinging at him with his lightning blades. Avani retrieved his sword, and was able to parry each blow, sending sparks flying through the air. Ash made one wrong move allowing Avani to grab his wrist and kick him in the chest. Ash flew a few feet away, landing hard, but he kept his footing; Avani brought his free hand up in a rising motion, causing the ground to unravel and wrap itself around Ash's legs, all the way up to his knees leaving him immobile.

Avani smirked, jumping in the air a few inches off the ground and disappearing upon his landing. He was swallowed by the dirt and a low rumble could be heard for a few seconds after which Avani popped up from behind Ash, bringing his blade around and putting the edge along Ash's throat.

"Okay," Ash said, "I surrender. You win."

"Of course I do. That was fun. I've had easier fights. Consider that a compliment."

"You call that a compliment?" Ash grumbled.

And with that Avani released the hold he had on the kid's legs, turned around, and walked away. He saw Quinn approaching as he left and heard her say to Ash, "I think he likes you."

He didn't hear what Ash said back but the Guardian wore a grin on his face as he left the training field.

Avani was thinking about how impressed he was. Maybe the kid had a decent chance of winning this fight for them. No one had ever taken Ozul down for good; he was a slippery snake, great at avoiding death for some reason. Ozul and his group of goons had tried several times to infiltrate and take down the

Guardians but had yet to succeed. The Guardians were only ever replaced for a couple of reasons, and it was usually due to old age. Sometimes, however, they were killed in battle, but Avani was certain none of the current Guardians would let that happen to each other.

There was a renewed hope born in Avani at that moment; perhaps one day this kid would bring peace to their world. For now, he would do his best to make sure Ash was ready for the coming battle.

Birkwood Park

They wrapped up training with the remaining time before the showdown with the Forbidden. The Guardians knew there was a chance they'd be outnumbered because their enemies didn't care about casualties, not even from their ranks. They couldn't risk taking the entirety of the Guild warriors; they would move on the enemy with only their best. Ash had to go, he was the person that Ozul was most interested in. Along with him, Quinn was another obvious choice. Her abilities with water were great and her chemistry with Ash was irreplaceable.

Then all four Guardians, their leadership would be valuable in the battle, plus their strength combined would be unmatched. The last member to be on the front line was Kane; he was the strongest and brightest pupil they'd seen in many years.

The whole group was set to meet in the center of the city beside the large fountain located near the Guild building. It's a large granite structure with a statue carving in the center of the very first Guardian. His name was Gabriel and was believed to be the first mage of Asmaria. No one knows how he came to be, but it is said that he could command a power unlike any other. There are stories told about his great feats such as defeating 100 enemies all on his own, using his weapon of choice which was the trident.

Ash sat in his house and said a prayer to the Great Tree for strength and courage to do what needed to be done. After it was done he felt silly. He was just a kid and a great amount was being asked of him; he did not wish to take life from anyone but knew it would most likely come down to that. He wasn't sure if he had what it takes to take another person's life and then remembered what he had done to Rick just a short time ago. He hadn't killed him but thought he did at first. He realized that no one in the Forbidden was someone he cared about and that seemed to ease his nerves a bit.

Ash left his house and then waited for Quinn to come out so they could walk together. When she emerged, she noticed him and said, "You didn't have to wait for me."

"I know," Ash told her, "I wanted to." He smiled as he stood up, reaching his hand out to her. She took it, interlacing their fingers as they began walking towards the rendezvous point. The sun was up in the sky and there was a gentle breeze, not much cloud cover to note. Ash thought how nice it felt, but knew that feeling would soon be over. They approached the fountain where the four Guardians waited for them along with Kane.

They all had somber looks on their faces, even Leena, who is usually chipper. Each of the fearless leaders had a gear bag filled with various weapons and first aid supplies. They greeted the young duo as they gathered up their belongings. Ash breaking the silence, asked, "How are we going to get there? Giant bird again?"

"You'll see," Bora said with a grin.

They walked down a path Ash had never ventured on before. It wound through the forest and up a small mountain. It wasn't nearly as tall as Frost Mountain. Halfway up the mountain were four large caves. As they climbed up to the cave openings the air turned more brisk. Brandr pulled out a small horn from the gear bag he carried and blew into it. The deep groan reverberated off the cave walls. The sounds following caused Ash to panic. Ash heard loud screeches and roars as whatever creatures within approached.

As the beasts got closer to the light, details started to appear. Ash could see the heads of four great serpents, each one a different color. No, these weren't just any serpents, they were dragons! Ash knew he shouldn't be afraid but he couldn't help it. He backed away, eyes locked on the beasts in front of him, and was almost to the ledge when Quinn grabbed his hand.

"Don't run." Quinn said, "It's okay, they won't hurt us. Remember when I told you Asmaria has all kinds of creatures? These are some of the older ones, and the most rare."

Leena sauntered over to the closest beast, laying her hand on its neck, and said, "Dragons used to roam all over Asmaria, but our past wars nearly wiped them all out. They haven't been used in a battle for a very long time, but we occasionally utilize them for transportation. These four have been carrying on the species, but they can only lay an egg once every hundred years. They have babies deeper in the cave system so hopefully they will continue to live on. We just have to make sure we protect them."

The blue dragon, which Leena patted on its massive neck, snorted, blowing lizard snot at Ash's feet. "This one," Leena said, "is Bulba. Just like water, he is powerful, with the strength of a thousand rivers."

"Kolora," Bora said, "White and gentle as the fluffiest of clouds." The white dragon nuzzled up to her, creating a sound similar to the purring of a cat.

Launching himself with a protruding chunk of rock, Avani landed on the back of the green dragon saying, "This is Iguru. His scales are as durable as the most solidified rock."

"And lastly," Brandr said, "This is Vesta. Her flames would rival even the magma found at the center of the Earth."

With the introductions of the dragons complete they all reared back on their hind legs and spewed a hot jet of flames into the air. Ash was in such a state of shock he didn't move or flinch, he didn't utter a sound, he just stood there with his mouth wide open and a look of bewilderment on his visage. Quinn looked at him and giggled, "What, first time seeing a dragon?"

Her voice snapped him out of the trance and he said, "Uh, yeah. Obviously. Who knew they were real?"

All of the dragons were relatively similar; they each had four legs, two wings, scales covering their whole body, and spikes running down their spines. Vesta was the largest of the four mystical creatures. Her size and power were amazing. The crew of warriors climbed up onto the backs of the beasts who bent their knees and launched themselves into the air with a few powerful flaps of their wings. Ash's hair whipped in the wind as they soared higher up into the sky. They moved toward New York at break-neck speeds.

Soon enough the landscape of New York came into their view. They stayed spread out far enough to where a single aerial attack wouldn't hit them all at once. As they approached Birkwood Park the dragons circled the area, searching for signs of their enemies.

After feeling sure that it was safe to land, Brandr who was on Vesta, looked at them and yelled over the roar of wind,

"Everyone ready?"

Ash and Quinn both nodded in response. Brandr yelled to get the other's attention who all gave a thumbs up, showing they were ready to go. "Let's go!" He yelled, as all four Guardians jumped off their winged rides. Quinn saw Ash's hesitation and grabbed his hand, pulling him with her as they tumbled off the back of Vesta.

Ash was too afraid to scream as they plummeted to the ground; he was sure they'd all be pancakes soon. As their bodies flailed he saw the dragons all circle one more time and turn back towards the direction they'd come from. He could see the adults had already made their way to the ground and were looking up at the falling kids. Before they reached their deaths Bora aimed her fists at them swinging them in small, tight circles creating a vortex of wind that slowed down their descent. This allowed them to land softly and safely instead of breaking every bone in their body.

Ash breathed sharply, "Someone could have warned me!"

"But where's the fun in that?" Bora said with a chuckle.

"Okay," Brandr said, his tone serious, "Keep your eyes peeled. They could be hiding anywhere. Let's take this slow."

They all crept through the park, fanning out into a wedge formation with Brandr in the front and Ash behind him to the right. They wound through the park slowly, making sure to be vigilant of their surroundings to not fall into any sort of trap.

Ash began thinking of Rick again. He thought he might try finding him after all this was over. Suddenly, as if being born from the shadows of the trees, there were roughly 100 men who appeared. They were dressed in all-black garments, the signature color scheme of the Forbidden. They formed a gaggle with three standing out in front. One of them Ash recognized as Juda, who stood there looking smug with a smirk on his face and his arms crossed over his chest. The one in the middle was Ozul for sure; he was a big man, well over six feet tall, and wore a gray emotionless mask to hide his features. The man on his other side sat on his knees, hands tied behind him, and a black bag over his head.

Ash's heart started pounding at an increased rate as he realized his father was there. He wanted so badly to talk to him or even just see what he looked like. He was so close to him and wanted nothing more than to save him from the clutches of this evil. Pulling the bow off his back, Ash nocked an arrow and screamed with rage, "Let my father go now!"

"Oh dear boy," Ozul said in his garbled voice, "How brave of you to think I'll just hand him over. Did you forget my offer? It's you, for him. Now, surrender your weapons, all of you. Or I will kill you all where you stand. Trust me, you're no match."

The Guardians, Ash, Kane, and Quinn spread out their V-shaped formation, giving themselves more room to fight. They all pulled out their weapons of choice; Brandr with his spear, Avani with his curved short sword, Bora using her chained mace, and Leena with a small dagger. Quinn preferred to not wield a weapon, but instead summoned water from thin air, forming it into tiny dart shapes. Ash already had his arrow aiming for Ozul, and Kane reached into his pouch, brandishing four throwing stars.

Ash saw him toss the throwing stars in the air. As the weapons dropped back down, he spread his hands slightly causing them to hover around him. Their sharp edges gleamed under the sun.

Laughing a deep, maniacal laugh Ozul said, "I was hoping you all would choose the more fun way of doing things."

The group of black-clad goons all laughed like hyenas and began preparing themselves for battle. "Ready boys?" Ozul asked as the dark members pulled out various weapons. Swords, knives, bows and arrows, spears. They began to circle the group of Asmarians. Ozul could be seen slinking back behind his men, dragging the bound man by his shirt collar.

Seeing his father being dragged sent a volt of anger through Ash. He Felt as if he were about to combust with rage; his eyes glowed like amethyst, and lightning ran up and down his body, arcing this way and that. A tendril of lightning worked its way down his arm and into the arrow that he had at the ready. All that was left was for him to find his target. He aimed in between the heads of the two villains furthest from him. Through that gap, he could see the back of Ozul stalking away. He loosed his electrified arrow which sent static through the air as it whizzed by.

Battle Hardened

Everything seemed to happen in slow motion for Ash as he let his deadly arrow fly. The arrow projected toward its target, zipping through the crowd. Just before it found its home Ozul spun around swinging his arm in a backward waving motion as he did so. A shadow sprung to life, engulfing the arrow and all of its power. The arrow disappeared for a moment and then Ozul waved the shadow away, leaving the arrow to drop on the ground, all of its potential gone.

Ash stared in amazement at how easily his enemy just swatted the most powerful attack he'd produced thus far like it was nothing. As the arrow touched down, all hell broke loose. The Forbidden began their assault, charging in like mad men. It was clear to Ash that they were not as powerful as the Guardians, but their anger and pain fueled them. It seemed as if they didn't care if they survived this, and that's what made them dangerous.

Ash watched in shock at the battle raging, and from the corner of his eye, he saw Ozul stalk up onto a large boulder where he sat to watch the chaos. He still wore that same mask he'd always been seen in, no expression to be read, no way to know what he was feeling at any given time. The bound man sat on his knees next to the boulder, trembling. Ash wondered if Ozul planned to just sit there until the end.

The guardians stood in front of the kids; spheres of darkness flew in from all directions, but they blocked them with their abilities. Spears flew, and arrows sailed by, all being blocked in some form or another. Ash fired off arrows, conserving his energy by not using the lightning to amplify them. Some of his shots were deflected and some landed on target nicely.

The first deadly thud that he heard made him feel sick. He watched as his arrow buried itself into a man's chest. He dropped his sword, fell to his knees and Ash watched from a short distance away as the life faded from his eyes. He choked the bile back down and continued to fight.

Every so often Ash would steal a glance at Quinn to see how she was doing. She would create tiny slivers of water that when flung at high enough speeds would tear through flesh. Any time an enemy got close enough she would whip water at them, cutting them up, or sometimes strangling them or forcing it down their throats to drown them.

Kane was fighting through enemies, trying his best to get to Juda. They certainly weren't making it easy for him. Juda focused on the white-haired prodigy, slinging shadowy spikes of death at him. Kane knocked each one to the side as he dropped foes left and right. His energy was faded faster than he thought it would.

Finally, he was standing a mere five or so feet from Juda who had a look of shock on his face. *Perhaps he has underestimated me*, Kane thought. The Forbidden Warrior tried to tackle Kane but he was prepared. Swirling inconspicuously above his head was a flurry of throwing stars. Just before Juda made contact, the deadly stars swooped down and sliced him along both arms.

He yelped and jumped back, then turned to attempt escape,

but Kane wasn't going to let him. He sent a gust of wind to trip the boy, and as he lay flat on his stomach, Kane lifted his right hand, causing the stars to change direction. They floated a few feet above Juda, waiting for Kane's command. With exaggerated force, he brought his hand down, sending the metal stars into Juda's body and ripping through the other side. His body jerked upon impact, and then became still, blood pooling underneath him as the life left him.

Kane breathed a sigh of relief after defeating Juda. He wasn't surprised though. As outnumbered as they were, Kane believed they were going to win. He stood watching as Brandr fought ferociously. He swept his arms from left to right, his flames taking on the form of a lion and striking down all in its path.

Avani was slashing with his sword in a fury. Two Forbidden shadows wrapped around his blades and ripped them from his hands. Kane was amazed as Avani stomped the ground with his feet. Causing the two enemies in front of him to sink up to their knees. He swung his palms facing out toward them, closed his fists, and then pulled his arms to his chest. The ground swallowed the two Forbidden henchmen and pulled them down under the Earth.

Kane watched as Leena and Bora fought side-by-side. They had both dropped their weapons and were using their elements to drop the foes before them. He regarded them as a great fighting pair, their wind and water often intertwining and working as one cohesive force.

Bodies lay strewn around the park, and blood leaked out, collecting beneath the ones on the ground. Those who were still alive lay on the ground groaning or screaming from pain. Ash saw Avani cleaning up; for each body, he walked past on the ground he would command the earth to swallow them up, whether they were still breathing or not, he didn't seem to care.

Ash panting fiercely looked at Quinn and yelled, "Hey! Are we winning?"

"I think so!" She responded, "We need to get around to Ozul now!"

"Not a chance girly!"

One of the Forbidden appeared from behind a tree and put Quinn into a choke hold from behind. His crooked smile made Ash rage; lightning began racing around his body.

"I'd simmer down if I were you," he said, "unless you want to see this knife go into your girlfriend's kidney." He poked a small, sharp knife into Quinn's side to get his point across.

Ash forced the lightning to subside, dropped his bow, and raised his hands in the air. "Okay, okay," he said, "What do you want me to do?"

"That's more like it. Ya see, my master over there wants you to join us for some reason. He thinks you are special, but me? I don't see it. I'm thinkin' we don't need you."

"Oh, would you just get on with it? You're starting to bum me out, loser."

With that, the man's smile faded and he put more pressure on Quinn's skin with his knife, drawing a thin bead of blood and releasing a whimper from her.

"Now now, don't go getting all smart with me. Here's what I want. I want you to get on your knees and beg me to spare her life. After that, I'll slit your throat, nice and slow."

Ash was thinking through any possible option in his head to get out of this. Everything he came up with ended with Quinn or himself dying. He hadn't known her for long, but she was his best friend, and it was obvious he had feelings for her even if he didn't know how to express them. He couldn't let anything happen to her while there was still breath in his body.

Ash slowly got to his knees and said, "Let her go. Now."

"Oh, Ash, that doesn't sound like begging." He jabbed his knife in further, drawing more blood and a loud squeal from Quinn.

"No," Quinn yelled, "Don't give him what he wants! Just kill him!"

Ash ignored her plea, "Let her go, please, I'm begging you! Just let her go and I'll let you kill me."

He shoved Quinn aside and she twisted her ankle as she fell to the ground. She yelped as she fell, clutching her injured ankle. Ash made a move to help her but only made it up to one foot when the man cut him off, pointing his knife at him.

"Oh no," he said, "I don't think so. Now then, lift your chin or she dies."

Without looking, he pointed his free hand at Quinn, a tentacle of darkness appeared, wrapping itself around her throat just enough to hold onto her without choking.

Ash knew what he had to do; he leaped into action by throwing a fast sweep with his foot trying to knock him off balance. The man jumped over his leg and lost concentration on his choking shadow hold.

Bora, who'd been fighting this whole time along with the others turned and noticed what was happening. She used a sweeping wind to gather up Quinn and move her to safety. Bora sent her behind a large tree and then followed to render first aid.

Ash was fighting with everything he had, his opponent was slashing and stabbing with his knife but was unsuccessful in landing any blows. Ash was throwing punches and kicks, knees and elbows. Sending confusing combos that landed almost every time. Blood poured from the guy's nose as Ash broke it with a sharp elbow to the face. Ash was enjoying this; he wanted to take him down as slowly as possible to revel in the victory. By the time he began using any shadow technique against Ash, he was too drained to do much. Ash easily avoided his attacks and then landed a devastating blow, a hard uppercut to the chin.

The man lay on the ground ultimately defeated by the boy. He breathed fast, shallow breaths. Tears welled in his eyes as he looked over and saw Ozul still sitting up on the large rock, not moving a muscle to help anyone. Ash looked over at Ozul, looked back at the enemy in front of him, and pointed his right palm at the enemy. He looked back at the Forbidden leader, anger rising in him, and created a blade of lightning that protruded out of his hand.

With all the opposing forces—except for Ozul—defeated, the Guardians turned to see what Ash was doing. They all breathed heavily, the exertion of the battle weighing on everyone. Ash pulled his arm back and just as he was about to thrust the lightning blade into the man's chest, Ozul stood up and yelled, "Wait! Don't do it. You win."

"Seriously?" Ash said, "You're not even gonna fight yourself? You're a coward!"

"I know!" Ozul fell to his knees off the rock and began sobbing. No, it just sounded like a sob at first, he was laughing. He threw his head back and laughed like someone losing their mind.

"Do you think I'd give up that easy?" He sent a massive shadow flying towards them, but it wasn't aimed at Ash. The curtain of shadow shifted to resemble a saw blade, just as it reached the prone man's neck. It sliced through, killing the man instantly. Ash couldn't believe what Ozul had just done.

"Wha-," Ash stuttered, "Why would you do that to one of your own?"

"You need not worry, my dear boy. For your battle has just begun."

Swan Song

Ozul yanked his gray mask off his face and shot a smirk over in the Guardian's direction who all had looks of surprise on their faces. He bent over and punched both fists into the ground causing it to split open in front of the Guardians. Walls of pitch-black darkness sprang out of the ground concealing him from their view. He dashed forward with superhuman-like speed, grabbed Ash by the collar of his shirt, and threw him into the middle of the makeshift battlefield.

As soon as Ash hit the dirt and rolled Ozul was already standing over him. He looked up, placed his hands together interlocking his fingers and his arms began to shake. The walls of darkness transformed into a dome around them, blocking off the outside world.

Ozul knew in his mind that he'd won. With the help of his dark master, Aros, his shadows were impenetrable for the amount of time he would need to break the boy. He didn't want to kill him, just break his spirit so that he would be easier to coerce. He was essential to their plan. It had to be him.

Ash was completely enveloped in darkness, his heart pounded in his chest, threatening to jump out of his rib rage. He could hear nothing but the sound of his ragged breathing and the scrape of his body on the ground as he rolled to his feet and stood up. He created a ball of lightning in each hand which gave him a bit of light to see by, but even that was mostly swallowed up by the darkness.

Ash couldn't see Ozul until the man had flames erupt from his hands. He was a few feet away, flinging orbs of fire around them, lighting the area up more than Ash's lightning.

Ash's eyes widened with shock, "Wait, I thought you could only control shadows."

Ozul laughed, "The amount of knowledge the Asmarians have on me is minute compared to what all I can do." His voice was still garbled, but less muffled without the mask on. Ash didn't know if it was just the darkness around them, but he swore that his eyes were just as pitch black as their surroundings.

The man had long brown hair, the same shade as Ash's. He had thick eyebrows, a thin scar cutting through the left one. His face was clean-shaven and he had a strong jawline. There was a familiarity about him that Ash couldn't piece together.

"Ash," he said, "Come with me. I know more about you than most others. I can unlock the greatness that lies dormant within you. Together, we could have anything we want."

"Oh yeah?" Ash replied, "And how would we get it? By force I presume? No, thanks. I don't want anything to do with someone who would steal, kill, and destroy just to get what they want."

"I thought you'd say that. You remind me a lot of myself when I was younger."

"I'm nothing like you."

"No? You don't feel ambitious? You don't have a void inside

you that can't be filled? You don't deal with rage that comes from nowhere?"

Ash was startled by how accurate this was. Ash had felt these things for as long as he could remember. "Okay," he said, "but still, there's a difference between feeling these things and acting on them. I would never hurt people to get my way. I have friends that I would never betray."

"Never? Not even for your daddy?" Ozul said as he waved his hand and a shadow materialized. Somehow Ozul had teleported the bound man from outside to inside the shadow dome.

There it was again. That burning rage. However, it didn't come from nowhere this time. That was his father sitting there, bound like an animal. No one deserved to be treated that way.

Lightning began coursing around through Ash's body at the sight of his tied-up father. He wanted to tear through this man, thing, or whatever he was. The moment before he could act on his impulses Ozul yanked the sack off the man's head revealing no one other than Rick Hampton.

Ash gasped at the sight of him and was wrought with confusion. Ozul just flung his head back and laughed, "You thought I had your real father? Your father is dead! How could you be so gullible?"

The fury inside Ash now was insurmountable; he wished for nothing but pain for Ozul. This time, Ash didn't feel apprehensive at the prospect of taking a life.

He looked at Rick intently. He had a gag over his mouth and a small cut surrounded by a green bruise under his right eye. He looked at Ash with fear in his eyes, trembling. Ash gave him a silent nod as if saying everything would be okay.

Then he rushed in to attack Ozul with a flying knee which he sidestepped effortlessly. Purple lightning surrounded his fists as he threw combo after combo at his opponent. Ozul blocked some but not all of the blows which were more powerful thanks to his ability. Ash wasn't giving him any sort of widow to respond with attacks of his own, he made him fight at his own pace which was full speed ahead.

Ash noticed that Ozul hadn't thrown a single blow of his own since this exchange started. His strikes began to slow down and he noticed a smile creeping up on the man's face. *Was this what he was waiting for?* Ash thought to himself. The lightning faded from Ash's fists and he slowed down to the point where he just stopped punching altogether and tried catching his breath. Ozul grinned. Ash looked over at Rick who had tears coming down his face and said, "I'm sorry".

"Well," Ozul said, "now that that's over, it's my turn." His smile got wider and he threw a straight push kick, connecting with Ash's chest and sending him flying into the dirt. He came at the boy with a barrage of attacks. With each strike, he laughed maniacally and let him recover just enough to feel the next shot.

Outside the dome, Kane looked at the gaping mouths of the Guardians. No one was saying anything and it was driving him crazy. Bora was feeding Quinn some heala in an attempt to heal her ankle faster.

"Anyone want to explain what's happening?" he asked.

For a moment he wondered if anyone was going to answer. Finally, Brandr began shaking his head slowly, "I don't know how this is possible. We thought Ash's father was dead up until the Forbidden Master said he had Augustus in captivity. To see him under that mask. I can't explain it."

"But," Leena said, "what do we do now? Ash is in there alone with him. We have to help him!"

Quinn interjected, "Can you guys please explain what's going on? I'm a little in the dark here, no pun intended."

Kane didn't consider himself to be a genius, but he figured out part of what Brandr was saying. "Ozul was just an alias. He wore the mask to hide his identity. That's Augustus, Ash's father."

Brandr nodded, "Right you are, Kane. There is a lot to unravel here. This begs the question, who is under that hood?"

Avani broke his silence, "We can figure all that out later. For now, let's get the kid out of there."

With that, they began working on the dome, firing each of their respective elements at it in succession to no avail. Avani parted the ground beneath and around the dome hoping to go underneath it, only to find that it was a full sphere. They tried everything in their arsenal of power to break into this thing but couldn't even make a scratch appear.

Inside the dome Ash lay on his back, broken and battered. Blood thickened the hair on his head and streamed from his nose. His lips were busted and one eye was swollen shut. He was fairly certain that a couple of his fingers had been broken and his legs ached as well.

He could hear Rick's muffled cries. A single tear crept out of his good eye and slid down his face. Ash reminisced about meeting Quinn and the Guardians, and all the other Asmarians he'd come across. He was glad to have made friends along this journey, even though he'd let them down in the end. He accepted his fate, this was the end for him, and he would die with dignity.

Ash rolled over and sat up on his knees as Ozul paced left and right in front of him, smiling as he did so. There was so much evil emanating from him, that Ash could feel it. Ash spat a mixture of blood and saliva from his mouth, looked up at Ozul, and said, "Go ahead. Finish it. I'm ready." He hung his head and closed his eye, ready for the final blow, but it didn't come. He looked back up at Ozul who just glared at him.

"I told you," he said, "I want you to come with me. I'm not going to kill you. You're coming whether you want to or not. See, I need you for the future. You will find that my plan for us is what's best."

"I wouldn't count on that. Honestly, I'd just rather you kill me."

"No, that simply will not do."

Ozul closed his black eyes, a shadow covered his body, and then stretched out on the ground towards Ash who was too tired to try getting away. The shadow enveloped him, closing him off from the world and as the light faded his whole body was chilled to the bone. When the darkness and cold released and light started to come back into view he noticed that he was in a different place. The light was dim, but he looked around with his good eye to find himself in what appeared to be a cave. The cave was large and he could see several members in black cloaks milling about.

He asked, "Where am I?"

"This," Ozul said, "is the Pit of Aros."

Ozul turned to discuss something with one of his minions and Ash took this moment to look around more, possibly for an escape route. He was in an area that was very large with high cave ceilings. There were tunnels lining the outer walls and some of the Forbidden members came in and out of them.

He even saw children coming in and out tossing around balls and playing tag.

"Now then," Ozul said as he turned back to Ash, "let's get you fixed up."

On his command, five or so of the Forbidden circled Ash and he prepared for an attack of some sort. They all thrust their hands forward and emitted what looked like a green shade, as it connected with and surrounded Ash's body he began to feel numb. The throbbing pain in his legs subsided, he watched his broken fingers mend and pop back into place, and eventually, his swollen eye reopened. He sat on the floor, looking at his hands and flexing his fingers, bewildered at what just happened. He had never been healed so fast in Asmaria.

"How did you do that? And why?"

"I told you," Ozul said, "I need you for my plans. We have the best healers here, although they can't leave the Pit, but that's no matter. Here." He reached out his hand to help Ash up.

Ash stood up without grasping Ozul's hand. This didn't change anything for him, they were still enemies, and he just had to figure out a way to escape. Ozul led him through one of the tunnels, it winded down into the earth for what seemed like ages. Every few feet there was a sconce on the wall with a flame burning. Ash never saw any detours out of this tunnel, it simply led from the large foyer area to wherever he was being taken. When they reached their destination the temperature had dropped at least twenty degrees and Ash shivered. They stood before a wooden door which was closed.

"After you," Ozul said, stepping aside and gesturing for Ash to open the door.

He swung the door open apprehensively, unsure of what lay in wait for him, but only found a small bedroom. There was a bed, a dresser, some desks, and a small bathroom. He found himself lost in curiosity, wondering how they were able to plumb this place.

Ozul said, "You will find a change of clothes in the dresser, and anything else you may need should be here. No reason for you to try leaving." He said the last line pointedly, hinting that he shouldn't try to escape.

"Ah, one more thing," Ozul said, pulling something from inside his robes, "can't be having you trying to fry anything with that lightning of yours." He pressed what looked similar to a gun into Ash's neck and pulled the trigger, shooting something deep into his skin.

"Ahh! What was that?" He exclaimed, which just made Ozul chuckle. "It's simply just a precaution." He turned and left the way he'd come, shutting the wooden door behind him.

Ash tried to summon lightning but found that he couldn't produce anything. *So that's what he meant. He blocked my powers with whatever that device was.* He searched through the dresser and all he could find was black clothing. It seemed like they were going to force Ash into looking like them too. He'd play along for now, perhaps cooperating would lead to an escape plan later down the road. He took a shower in his tiny bathroom and got dressed in some pajamas that consisted of a black, long-sleeved shirt and black cotton pants. He laid down, exhausted from the day's events, and had a night of restless sleep.

The Guild Meeting

As the black dome disappeared, Kane readied himself to attack. Wind whirled around his hair. He dashed forward and summoned a gust to carry him over the fading wall of black as it receded into the ground. He landed swiftly but the bound man was all that remained. Kane looked at him with a lone eyebrow raised. The hood had been pulled off his head.

Brandr, followed by the other Guardians and Quinn who was hobbling, strode up to the man. He carefully removed the gag from his mouth.

"State your name."

"Rick Ham— Hampton."

"Why were you with that man? Why was he pretending that you were the boy's father?"

"I am his father. Or was I guess."

"We know who you are to Ash, we just don't understand the charade."

Kane didn't detect anything suspicious in Rick. He knew—from talking to Ash—that Rick had found him as a baby and rescued him. He was also unsure of why Augustus would fake this scenario.

Rick took a few slow breaths and then said, "All I know is that man claimed to be Ash's real father. He told me that he would use me to get close to him. Whenever I would ask questions, they would…"

He couldn't finish his sentence through the sobs that issued.

"They would beat you." Kane finished the thought for him.

"Yes, that's exactly right." Rick nodded as the tears washed over the wounds on his face.

Brandr asked, "Did you get any sort of insight as to where their lair is held? This could help us dearly in retrieving Ash and defeating this group of evildoers once and for all."

"I'm sorry, I only ever saw the inside of a cell."

Bora walked over and cut the bind on his wrists and pulled him into an embrace, combing his hair with her hand. "Everything's gonna be okay. We won't let them hurt you again."

The Guardians discussed quietly in a tight circle as to what the next steps should be. Quinn sat on a bench with Rick making small talk. Kane could hear Quinn filling him in on what happened after Ash attacked him not that long ago. Rick blamed himself for letting things get out of hand with Ash. He showed them the web of red scars on his chest from the lightning that had only just healed.

The Guardians checked the bodies of the slain enemies for anyone who may still be alive, gathering up the survivors. Avani buried the dead deep into the Earth where no one would find them. They called the dragons back to their location and hopped onto their strong, scaly backs, and headed back towards Asmaria.

Kane was stymied by not being able to penetrate the shadow dome that Augustus created. He wasn't keen on looking inadequate. It was during such an important moment too. Had he broken through, Ash would be with them and Augustus may have been defeated. He still wasn't strong enough.

Upon their return to Asmaria, Brandr called a Guild meeting to begin within the hour so that they could update everyone. They all met in the meeting hall and filled the auditorium-style seating. Quinn couldn't help but wonder if there would have been a different outcome had they taken more of the Guild members with them. She was mortified that Ash was taken.

Brandr's booming voice interrupted her thoughts, "Thank you all for gathering in haste on such short notice. We wanted to debrief you as to what transpired during the battle at Birkwood Park. You probably have noticed by now that Ash is not standing here with us." There were murmurs among the crowd, no doubt assuming the worst. He continued, "Now, as far as we know he is still alive. The leader of the Forbidden was much stronger than we previously thought. It appears he can teleport using shadows, and was able to sidetrack the rest of us while he abducted Ash. We don't know what his intentions are with him, but we know they can't be good. The other part we want to divulge, the man known as Ozul is someone we believed to be dead. His real name is Augustus, Ash's real father."

Chatter erupted throughout the auditorium; the Guardians tried to silence them but were having no luck. The mages simply couldn't believe what they had just heard. Avani stretched his arms wide and clapped his large hands together, causing the ground to rumble which grabbed the attention of the crowd. After calming down, Avani said, "Now then, we know you all have questions, and so do we. As of now, we have the same knowledge as you. None of us know how this could be possible. We believed Augustus to be dead just as his wife was, and this was a shocking revelation to everyone. If any of you have even an inkling of an idea as to how he is alive and leading the Forbidden please don't hesitate to come forward, even if you must do so in private."

"With that," said Brandr, "We are all very exhausted and in need of rest. We will go ahead and conclude this meeting. Tomorrow morning we will meet again to go over some action plans as to what to do next. Rest assured, we will get Ash back at any cost. If you're uncomfortable with that statement I won't hold it against you. I'll just remind you, Ash, a boy who is brand new to our world just sacrificed himself for the rest of you."

That statement left the other mages silent, there was nothing else to be said. The Guardians spoke quietly among themselves while the others made their exit. Quinn was the last to leave the auditorium. She retired to her home and broke down the day's events to her parents. She spared no detail, and when she finished she let herself break down, tears streaming down her cheeks. Her mother hugged her tightly while her father kissed her on her head.

Storms of lightning, fire, and darkness raged in his head, Ash felt helpless in his own mind. The nightmare was unrelenting causing his body to thrash in the small bed. In the dream he was running while lightning crashed around him, threatening to smite his body. Flames poured from the sky, igniting everything around him, smoke filled his lungs as he gasped for air. Tendrils of darkness threatened to smother the life from him.

His body was flung from the bed, and he landed flat on his back on the hard, rocky floor of his new living quarters. He awoke on impact, the air leaving his lungs, he heaved on the ground clutching his chest.

Once his breath had returned he gathered himself up, noticing that his shirt collar had a ring of sweat, so he decided to change clothes. After washing up and changing he knew he wasn't going to be able to get any rest that night. He slipped on his shoes and put on a black cloak and pulled the hood on over his head.

Ash was surprised to find that the door was unlocked; he wound his way back toward the corridor he entered through. The sconces were all still lit with the flames dancing around as if alive. Before walking out into the foyer he stopped to listen for voices. Hushed tones were heard but he could not make out what was being said. He pressed forward, looking up to see two men in a deep conversation, and the one whose face could be seen made eye contact with him.

"Going somewhere?" he asked.

"Nah. Anywhere to get a bite to eat at this hour?"

The second man turned to Ash, revealing a large scar across his face. He grumbled, "What makes you think we're gonna give you food, boy?"

"Please sir, would you be so kind as to feed a poor, starving boy?" Ash asked facetiously. And then added, "Mr. Scarface?" Ash meant to insult him. He jumped up from the table, whirled around, and reached his hand out, causing a shadowy hand to appear and wrap around Ash's throat.

"I will end you where you stand, boy," the man spit with venom in his voice.

"Argo," the other one said, placing his hand on the man's shoulder, "That's enough. Let him go. You know how Lord Ozul will feel about this."

Argo released his hold, turned, and stalked away, the tail of his cloak flapping with his brisk pace. He grumbled something that Ash couldn't hear.

"I'd be careful around here if I were you. This isn't Asmaria where everything is rainbows and sunshine. This is the Pit of Aros. Darkness and death dwell here. You'd be better off to not forget that." The mysterious fellow turned around and exited down one of the many tunnels that branched off from the main cavern.

Well, I guess it's time to explore, Ash thought to himself. The foyer was sort of oval-shaped, massive, and had nothing but tunnel entrances every few feet. There were more sconces on the walls here with flames, but the place was so large that the light was still fairly dim. Wooden tables and chairs were scattered about in no specific pattern, like what could be found in a pub from TV.

He picked a tunnel that was directly in front of him, about 30 feet away. He slowly opened the door and peered in, there was nothing but darkness that met his eyes. He went back and broke a leg off one of the wooden chairs, tore off a piece of his cloak, and lit it with one of the burning wall torches. Ash crossed the threshold and slowly closed the door behind him.

Broken

Quinn had never felt so hollow; she had never lost anyone important to her before now. She wasn't sure what Ash was to her or what she was to him, but she knew that she cared for him deeply. She hadn't ample time to process everything that transpired in the past couple of days. She took multiple lives the prior day, fighting with everything she had to protect Asmaria and Ash.

This was Quinn's first real battle; it was a bit different than what her teenage brain previously thought. She didn't expect it to be so hard to process killing other people. After making it back to her house, she showered and scrubbed herself frantically, as if the death was stuck to her. Plopping down to the floor of the shower, she pulled her knees in, hugging her legs, and let the water wash over her. She felt broken inside.

There was no way for her to know for sure that Ash was alive, but she had to believe that he was still out there fighting. She had to believe it because if she didn't then she may as well give up being a warrior altogether. Warriors were meant to be strong and fearless. What was she? A weak, weeping, little girl who was in way over her head.

Quinn wanted so badly to be the one to find Ash and bring him home. It didn't matter that he wasn't born in Asmaria, this was his home now. She wished she had told him how she felt, but now it was too late. She assumed he most likely knew how she felt, and reciprocated those feelings, but she needed to speak them aloud so that there would be no doubt between them. Negative thoughts swarmed her mind all night, and no matter what she did, her mind tormented her.

Quinn walked around, mindlessly wandering as she poured over every possible avenue in her mind that could lead to rescuing Ash. Her muscle memory leads her to the training field. She didn't notice where she was until the familiar sounds of swords clashing, arrows landing, and the symphony of elements filled her ears.

She looked up and her eyes found Kane's. He was walking toward her. She remembered the days when she had a crush on him. She thought he may have liked her too, but then they grew apart and she was content with being friends.

"How you holding up?" he asked.

She lied, "I'm good. What about you?"

"I can't help but think that it's my fault. I should have been stronger. I should have found a way inside that dome."

"I don't think it was anyone's fault except for the people responsible for taking him."

"That's a mature way of thinking."

She nodded. The noise was beginning to irk her. She motioned for him to follow and they walked out of the field and found a bench to sit on away from the commotion of those training.

She said, "I lied. I'm not good."

He chuckled softly, "Yeah, I kind of figured that. I know you pretty well."

Quinn couldn't contain herself any longer. Her hands met her face as she tried to hide her tears and began sobbing. She felt like a silly girl. Crying over a boy that she had only known for a short time. In front of a boy that she used to have a crush on. She felt Kane's arms wrap around her and pull her in tight. She didn't realize it until now, but this is exactly what she needed.

"It's going to be okay. We're going to find him." Kane tried to reassure her.

It worked. After holding their embrace for a couple of minutes he let go. She pulled away and wiped her face. The sky was blurry through her burning eyes.

"Thanks," she told him. "I needed this."

He smiled that brilliant smile that she used to love, "Me too."

They bid each other farewell and he went back to the training field. She knew it was his home away from home. Quinn wasn't sure where she would go but knew that she didn't want to sit at her house.

Quinn was feeling much better. Her mind felt more solid. She was resolved to figure out a way to bring Ash home. He was the most important thing in her life now.

Ash was the best friend she's had in a long time. Quinn wasn't particularly good at making friends; she was nice to everyone for the most part, but the other girls her age weren't interested in training consistently every day. She couldn't make time to be a girly girl like the others, she wanted to become strong and there was only one way to do that.

Quinn never wanted to feel this way again, she began thinking about where this lair could be. Rick had told them that he was in a cave somewhere. There are millions of cave systems all over the world and they could be in any one of them. Then she remembered how it seemed that Augustus could teleport; it only made sense that it would take loads of energy to teleport far distances.

She assumed that they couldn't be on the other side of the world. It would be too much for him to handle teleporting that far.

Quinn went to bed and attempted to sleep. It took at least an hour, maybe longer, for her mind to finally quiet and shut down. She had wonderful dreams that night about walking across the Asmarian beaches, hand in hand with Ash.

Demon King

Ash was chilled to the bone as soon as he stepped into the dark. Most of the light from his torch was swallowed by the darkness. He walked slowly and tentatively, holding the torch out as far as possible from his body in an attempt to cast the light. It got colder the further he walked. The flame got smaller until eventually burning out, but at that point, he could see a dim blue light ahead. Curiosity gripped him like a vice. He approached and heard voices, his nerves began to spike and he wasn't sure why.

The sight he saw struck him as odd. In the very center of the square room was an obelisk that appeared to be around six feet tall. It had weird engravings covering it in a pattern that spiraled from the bottom to the top. There were precious gemstones all around the base that appeared to glow faintly blue. Just on the opposite side of this obelisk was Ozul, standing before a black figure who resembled a man, but was completely black, devoid of any other color, except his eyes. He appeared to have bright yellow eyes but that was the only part of his body that wasn't darkness. He didn't look like a shadow as Ozul did the first time they met, but just innate darkness. The man sat on a throne that shifted in patterns of grays and dim whites, faces swirling along its surface. Whatever this thing was it was the epitome of evil. Ash crouched down slowly, trying to eavesdrop without drawing attention to himself.

The dark man's voice had a calming effect on Ash even though he wasn't being spoken to as if it were inviting him in, it was soothing in a way that also made Ash uncomfortable.

"Where is the boy now?"

Ozul paced around the obelisk with his hands behind his back. Ash could see his eyes in the blue-flamed torches lining the chamber walls. The blackness had left them and they shone amber with green flecks."He sleeps in one of the cave rooms, my liege."

"Good. And what of the Guardians?"

"They, uh.. escaped."

"What?" The thing yelled, the nature of his voice changing from soothing to venomous.

"What did I tell you about failing me, Augustus?"

"Augustus?" Ash blurted out the question without thinking. He forgot that he was just trying to listen without being caught, but that name threw him off. That was the name of his father, but he was dead, wasn't he? The two men turned in unison to the boy, Augustus standing.

Ash tried to turn and run, but as soon as he did, a tentacle of darkness wrapped around his body, it squeezed the air from his lungs. The shadow picked him up off the ground and carried him towards the dark figure. He noticed that the tendril was coming from the man's mouth, which was gross as far as he was concerned. He squirmed against the force until it dropped him to the floor just a few feet away from the beast where he gasped for air.

"Eavesdropping are we?" The man spat the question as if he had a bad taste in his mouth. "How dare you enter my chamber uninvited."

"You- you're Aros aren't you?"

"Ah, so you aren't as dumb as you appear, eh? Tell me, what do you know about me?"

"Well, I only read a brief story about the Forbidden and Asmarians in a battle. After interrogating some of their captives, they found that you're the source of the others' power."

"That's where you're wrong," the inviting nature of Aros' voice returned, "this here is my obelisk. It's older than I am, and you do not want to know my age, I assure you. This is where their power comes from. You see, I can only possess one person at a time. Not very useful is it? No, I had to come up with some other way of dispersing my energy so that the others can get a little taste of it."

"Why are you telling me all this? If you're gonna kill me then stop wasting my time and get on with it." Ash said with indignation.

Augustus made a step forward as if to strike Ash, but Aros held up his hand, signaling for him to stop. "I would never kill you, dear boy, I need you." He grinned with a toothless smile.

"I keep hearing that. What do you need me for exactly?"

"Well, now that is the question, isn't it? I've been waiting for you for thousands of years. It dates back to when we demons roamed the galaxies at free will when humans would worship us. They called us Gods! I'm the last of my kind." He became angry as he continued, the heat from his flaming throne became more intense. "My brothers and sisters all perished because of humans. But do I hold it against you all? No, I pity you. You're all weak. I will lead humanity as their king, into a new world."

Aros sat back down, crossing his legs, and continued with his story, "There was a fable about a boy who would be born into this world on a lightning bolt. He would possess the power to save this world or rule it as its master. Your father here," Aros looked between the two, "has been a great addition to my army. You were born on a night when lightning rained down from the skies in greater numbers than ever before. You are that boy from the story, I know it to be true. With you, we will take over and rule this world, make it in our image, make it better than anyone has ever dreamed!"

Ash let this revelation of information collect in his mind. His real dad stood before him, just a few feet away. And yet, he hated him. He could see the physical resemblance in the two of them and hated that this was the father the universe gave him. He took a deep breath to collect himself and respond to Aros.

"And how exactly are we gonna do that? Enslave mankind? Kill those that stand in our way? I don't think so, you'll have to kill me, I'll never work for you."

Aros chuckled, stood up, and faced Augustus who spread his arms making the T shape; Aros stepped up to him and kept walking, and his body dissolved into Augustus.

His voice became more distorted, "You see, I don't need your cooperation. I'll possess you and you'll have no choice." The shadowy demon stepped back out of Augustus, "With our combined powers we will destroy the Asmarians and then this planet will be mine for the taking. I will be the King of this world!"

"I will not let that happen!" Ash turned to his father, "How could you do this? You were an Asmarian, one of the good guys! And what about my mom, did you kill her too?"

A look of remorse crossed Augustus' face but fled just as quickly. Before he could answer the questions the demon interrupted, "Augustus, take this brat back to his quarters and ensure he doesn't come into my lair uninvited again. Make it painful for him."

Augustus touched his hand to the obelisk for a brief moment and when he pulled it away a small stream of darkness followed, soaking into his hand. He grabbed Ash by the back of his collar and dragged him back down the long hallway from which he'd come. Ash tried to break the grip, but his fist was closed too tight. Once they got back to his room Augustus shoved him into the floor where he bounced back up quickly, expecting a fight.

Ash hoped he'd get close enough, but he just said, "Listen, I'm not going to hurt you. Not yet anyway. But you have to promise me that you won't go back in there."

"You never answered me. What did you do to my mother?" Ash's eyes welled with tears, but he refused to let them spill over. "How could you let this thing live? You could kill him!"

"No! You do not understand what you speak of. There is no killing him, there is only co-existence. You will obey and do as he says, or I will murder everyone you care about."

He turned and left the room, this time locking the door behind him. Ash was left with his jaw dropped, wondering how this man who was his father could be so heartless. Was he destined to enslave the world as a puppet to this demon?

Rick Hampton rested in a hospital bed where he was fed heala and given water and electrolytes to replenish what he'd lost. In his time as a captive, he was not only tortured but starved as well. Most of his muscle mass was gone and he had very little fat left as well. The nursing staff was very kind to him.

Rick was feeling better already. The nurses there didn't tell him what the little cubes he was munching on were made of, but it was doing the trick. He was wondering where the TV was; there was nothing for him to do but sit and wait. He was feeling antsy. Luckily Quinn showed up.

"Hey, you want to come to a Guild meeting? They're supposed to talk about what the next plan of action with Ash is."

This was great news for Rick. "I'd love that. This place is getting old. Just let me get dressed."

Quinn left the room to wait in the hall while Rick gathered his stuff up. He still couldn't believe everything that had happened. Rick was both elated and stricken with fear at the sight of Ash. He missed him dearly, despite what he'd done to him the last time they were together. Rick knew that his injuries were his fault. He should have kept his emotions in check.

Rick didn't consider himself a skeptic but, he also never would have imagined that there was a whole group of people with the ability to control elements. It was like something out of a superhero movie. They brought him here on the back of a dragon. Who knew those were real?

Rick overheard someone talking about a Guild meeting that would be happening soon. He gathered that the Guild was their fighting class of citizens. He didn't know how long they would allow him to stay here, but he was determined to help in any way he could.

Quinn brought Rick to the auditorium where they found a seat amongst the sea of Guild members. They watched as all the Guardians but Avani entered the room.

Brandr spoke, "Asmarian warriors, I'm here to bring you all an update on the current situation. As I speak, Guardian Avani is interrogating the prisoners we brought back with us from the battle. We are hoping he will be able to divulge some useful information from them. Prepare yourselves for the dark days ahead, for weakness will only bring misfortune to us all.

"As your leaders, we have discussed in depth about what our next actions will be. We will not rest until we crush our enemies beneath our feet forever. It is no secret that the majority of the Forbidden is made up of Asmarians who were born powerless so from this point forward we will be keeping a close eye on them. Do your duty to Asmaria and prevent any more of them from betraying our land."

Concluding his speech, Brandr turned around, making room for Leena to step forward. He took his seat and let her address the Guild. "My fellow people, believe me when I say, those evildoers will pay for what they've done. At this point, we still don't know anything more about Augustus and how he has been alive this entire time." This statement caused a lot of grumbling and murmuring among the crowd.

"Actually," Avani, who'd entered unnoticed, walking up to the stage interjected, "I have concluded my investigation with our inmates. I was able to acquire a few secrets that they tried to keep from me, however, I'm not sure how useful the information will be in rescuing Ash." Quinn leaned forward in her seat.

Avani continued, "I found the weak link of the four prisoners and was able to get out of him why they want Ash so dearly. It's been right under our noses this whole time. Many of you may remember the old prophecy of the boy who would save or enslave the world." Most of the crowd nodded their heads, Quinn was one of the few who was dumbfounded with no knowledge of this tale.

"For those of you who are ignorant of this story, I will tell you;

the Great Tree once told that a boy will be born of lightning, he will grow into a fierce warrior, and will be the savior of this world or will enslave it's people as he reigns master of all. They believe that this boy is Ash. It was revealed to me that Augustus is not their sole master. Aros lives. He commands their forces through Augustus."

Quinn stayed in her seat—though shocked—while havoc exploded around her. The Guild members erupted, many of them jumping to their feet, shouting over one another. There was no sense to be made of the chaos, they were all coursing with fear. Everyone in Asmaria had heard of Aros, but many believed him to be vanquished long ago. No one has spoken that name apart from telling stories in many years.

"Silence," Avani yelled repeatedly until calm broke over the people, "I know this seems crazy. But I can't think of anyone else who could possibly give this group of people such power. I've no reason to believe it's a lie. Augustus vanished before our eyes, and let's not forget, he used to be a very powerful fire mage. Why would he turn to the darkness? It just doesn't make sense unless someone more powerful was goading him."

Brandr arose from his seat. He asked Avani directly, but loud enough for everyone to hear, "Was there any sort of information about their location?"

"I did get something, although, it's vague. One of them taunted me, saying that our arrogance blinds us to what's right in front of us. He said Asmaria wouldn't stay on top for long and that one day soon we would find ourselves on the bottom of the ocean."

Leena stood up to her feet, "What if that means they're a lot closer than we ever thought? Maybe they have been deceiving us to believe that their hideout is farther away than we would ever expect."

This train of thought was the same that Quinn had!

Bora asked, "What are you saying?"

"Well we know that they would hide in a very dark place, like a cave, and there are plenty of caves around the island. So what if their lair is somewhere on Asmaria?"

"Asmarians," Brandr addressed everyone once more, "We will begin searching at once. Scour every inch of this island, if you find anything suspicious, anything that could lead us to them you are to signal for the rest of us. Gather some gear and go at once!"

Ready for action, the Guild dispersed from the building quickly to get ready for the search. The Guardians said farewells to each other and parted ways, heading back to their abodes to gather supplies and get ready for the search party. They already wasted a whole day, and time was of the essence.

Quinn turned to Rick, "We have to go. I'll show you to Ash's house and you can wait there."

She jogged out of the building with Rick close behind. She showed him to Ash's home and then darted inside her own. Just before she reached the door, there was a wooshing sound overhead. She looked up to see Kane using gusts of wind to carry himself through the air to his house.

Crawling Things and Dark Beings

Kane moved as quickly as possible; using wind to carry himself could become tiresome but he figured he would have enough time to recover before anything crazy happened. He packed a gear bag and then headed back in the direction he'd come from. He dropped down to the street just as Quinn exited her home.

"Hey," he said, "Wanna head out together?"

"Sure, but don't plan on slowing me down." She gave him a wink.

Kane laughed, "Yeah right, just try to keep up."

They walked through the streets of the city, heading towards the outskirts. Just before they reached the jungle Kane saw Rick sneaking in ahead of them. He nudged Quinn and pointed. The man looked around as if checking to see if he was being followed but didn't see the two kids.

They gave a look to each other that said it was odd to see him walking around out here by himself, heading in the same direction as everyone else. They followed him discreetly. Kane used the wind to carry them slowly, although he had to let them down every so often to regain his energy.

They watched him creep through the jungle for about a mile and then stop. He looked around and then began dry heaving.

After a few seconds, something started wriggling out of his mouth.

The kids watched in horror and disgust as a large black centipede-looking creature, at least ten inches long, crawled its way out of his gullet. It flopped on the ground and then scurried off into the bushes. Rick promptly collapsed and the two ran over to him.

"What the heck was that?" She asked, but Kane just shook his head; speech was suddenly evading him. She shook Rick and after a few shakes he came to, looking confused.

He sat up, looking around to see the surrounding jungle, "How did I get out here?"

"You really don't remember anything?" she asked.

"No, why? What happened?"

"Well, we saw you sneaking out here, looking suspicious so we followed. And then you came to this spot and…"

"And what?"

Kane said, "Uh, you kinda puked up this huge centipede thing."

Rick laughed, "You're kidding right?"

The two just stared at him in silence.

"Oh of course you aren't." He just shook his head.

Quinn said, "Listen, I think we should just get you to the hospital. Just in case."

Kane left Quinn who agreed to wait for him. He summoned gusts of wind to carry himself and Rick who squealed with either glee or terror, he wasn't sure which. They made it back to the hospital and explained to the staff what happened. They decided it would be best to cuff Rick to the bed this time and he seemed to have no apprehension to that.

Ash paced in worried thought, he needed to figure out a way to get out of there. He had an idea and began feeling his neck to see if there was anything he could do to get his powers back. He found a lump, roughly the size of a black-eyed pea. Now he just needed to figure out a way to extract the device.

He searched around the room and in one corner there was a small, pointy rock. He began to put pressure on his flesh, careful not to press too hard into his carotid artery. Blood started trickling out over the stone and his fingers, getting them wet and sticky, he continued until he was able to get the small device out. It plopped out and hit the floor, and he realized he was holding his breath. He let it out, feeling a bit light-headed, but he knew he needed to act fast.

He summoned a small, focused, arc of lightning from his index finger and ran it across his neck wound, cauterizing it. It hurt quite a bit, but it was necessary. He had to escape before that demon took over his body. He blasted the locked door open and fled down the cave hallway. Before he entered the open area he checked around the corners to see if anyone was there, but he saw no one.

There was no helping the temptation. Ash wanted to get one more look at the demon king. He fled down the hall, this time without a torch. His footsteps were almost silent. He dragged his fingertips across the walls to help make sure he didn't trip. When the dim blue light came into his view he slowed down and regained control of his heavy breaths. He peered into the chamber; there was a small clear ball in Augustus' hands and images flashed by as a camera seemed to be slithering across the jungle floor. But modern technology doesn't work here.

"It worked, master." He heard his father say. "This was the perfect spy tool."

The evil being laughed jovially. "No one would ever suspect that oaf of a human to have something like that inside of him. Now we just wait for the visupede to get into position. We'll be able to see the Asmarians coming and they won't see the ambush coming.

He'd heard enough. Ash turned and bolted down the hallway. Once back into the main corridor, he chose a tunnel at random. Behind it contained nothing but barrels of something that smelled like spoiled food.

He turned and took a chance on one of the closer tunnels, entering before anyone caught him. He was smacked in the face with a foul stench, making him think that this is what rotting meat must smell like, and heard terrible sounds that had to belong to some sort of wicked beast. He quickly exited and picked another tunnel. He opened the door and stepped inside; the initial entrance was short and led to a tall ladder.

This has to be the way out! He thought to himself as he began to climb. He couldn't see the top of the ladder, but there was a dim light up there so he pushed on. Climbing began to take its toll on him, his arms burned and his back muscles screamed for a break.

With each rung he felt that he was closer to escape so he continued to climb. Below him Ash could hear shouts, so he assumed they noticed he was getting away, however, there was no hand of darkness reaching out of the shadows to pluck him back down.

After what seemed like an eternity, the top of the ladder was finally in view. Just a few more rungs and he was home free. Ash made it to the top where he just sat on the edge, catching his breath and letting his aching muscles cool off. The shouts from below were still echoing throughout the chamber but he figured they'd be far enough behind him that he could rest for a couple minutes. There was a big metal door with a small window letting sunlight shine through. After resting for a while he got up, excited to be free, he tried opening the door.

Locked, he shook the door violently, cursing under his breath. He wasn't sure if he'd be able to blast through a metal door like he could a wooden one. Ash gave himself a few calming, deep breaths and began to work. He created a steady stream of lightning bolts aimed at the middle hinge. After a few minutes, the hinge had finally melted away so he started in on the other two.

Quinn and Kane roamed around the jungle slowly, to be efficient and not miss anything. Every so often they would come across another Guild member and ask if they had seen anything, but none had. Using the wind, Kane would float above the trees to see if anyone was signaling for backup yet. Kane suggested going toward the center of the island, "I don't know why, but something is pulling me in that direction. And since the Great Tree is there, I think we had better check it out."

Quinn reluctantly agreed and they trekked their way up to the tree. Soon enough, their life-giving tree came into view; it was as lustrous as always, its bright flowers and leaves blooming. Kane was right, something did feel a bit off about the holy grounds, but she didn't know what it was yet.

Quinn wanted to signal for the others but thought it best to wait for some concrete proof that something was going on here. They searched around the base of the tree methodically, moving fallen leaves and brush out of the way, looking for anything that could be an entrance. After searching for a while she heard Kane yell, "Over here!"

Kane was roughly 30 meters away, looking at the ground. Quinn jogged over to where he stood; he explained that he was using small gusts of wind to move leaves and foliage around to completely check the ground.

That's when he noticed a large rock shimmy in a way that was unnatural and decided to see if he could move it. To his surprise, the rock was very light and he was able to flip it over where he could see that it was hollowed out and underneath was a circular, metal door. It was locked from the inside which they discovered upon trying to open it.

Standing in this spot, she could see what was off about the Great Tree; almost as if it was pointing to the area they were standing on, the branches on this side were gathered up, twisting up into each other. The tips of the limbs hovered near their heads, with a singular black flower, pulsating. She never noticed it before, the tree must have known what was going on, and it wanted to help.

They decided to signal for the others at that point, they'd found the entrance, but no one would have thought it would be this close to the tree. Kane pulled the signaling horn from his pack and blew into it. Quinn could feel the sound vibrating in her chest. The Guardians arrived and they explained what was found.

Ashes

Finally melting off the last door hinge, Ash took a second to catch his breath, the smell of burning metal filling his nostrils. His stomach rumbled, reminding him how very hungry he was and he couldn't remember the last time he'd eaten. After regaining some strength he gave the metal door a hard kick.

It flung open and hit the ground, stirring up dust. Ash noticed that the light emanating from the doorway wasn't sunlight at all, but rather a single bulb hanging from a high ceiling. It looked brighter to him from being in this cave, he wasn't accustomed to the dark. Next to it was a metallic circle with a rope ladder under it, which he bet was a door. The thing Ash failed to notice was the person lurking in a dark corner, watching his every move.

Deep laughter rang out and creeping out into the light was Augustus. "Did you *really* think we would just let you escape? How foolish do you think we are?"

Ash was confused. How did they get here so fast? The confusion faded into anger.

It welled up inside him as he stared into those cold, black eyes and wished nothing but pain for his father and the demon inside him. With a roar he attacked, arcs of purple lightning sprang forth from his hands but were met with a stream of shadow from Augustus, nullifying it. They both charged each other, Ash flinging bolts at Augustus who countered each one. The fight went to hand-to-hand combat and Ash was able to get his hands on his opponent, who just smiled. It was an evil, knowing smile as if he had a secret about to be discovered.

He growled, "You shouldn't have made contact with me, boy."

Before Ash could let go, tendrils of darkness reached out of his father's body and began wrapping themselves around his arms. He was able to let go but the shadows kept their hold; he started taking backward steps and the shadow followed, being pulled out of Augustus' body.

Aros' face, with his bright yellow eyes, appeared. Once the demon fully emerged, laughing the entire time, he merged with Ash, sinking into his pores, and taking over his body. The world went dark inside of Ash's mind. However, after a moment his vision returned. He could see his father on his knees.

It was like looking through a window made of smoke. He couldn't make out all the details through the haze, but he could see enough. Ash couldn't feel anything physically. He watched one of his hands lift as lightning, now black as the night, arced from him to Augustus.

Augustus squirmed beneath the shock and once it subsided he fell over, unconscious. Ash could hear Aros breathing. He felt what Aros felt. A feeling of pure elation. He had never felt so powerful in all his time.

Aros spoke in their shared mind, "Finally. The perfect vessel."

Ash screamed, "GET OUT OF MY BODY!"

"Silence!"

And then Ash couldn't get another word out.

Aros, using Ash's body like a puppet, bent down and reached

into one of Augustus' pockets. He pulled out the glass ball, peered into it, and revealed that the Asmarians were already at his doorstep. They stood on the ground above him, just a few feet away, attempting to break into the lair. Images flashed through Ash's brain as the demon pictured himself rolling around in the carnage that he was about to create.

Above the ground, Kane could hear an intense battle erupting below their feet. It was no doubt Ash and someone else. Screams and the clash of elements were evident. The Guardians began attempting to open the door; they bashed it and pried, but it wouldn't come loose. They were too scared to split the ground open in fear of damaging the tree because of how close it was. Brandr began blasting the door with fire, turning it orange. He stopped abruptly, there was a loud banging coming from the inside and a voice could be heard yelling, "Stop! Stop! I'm coming out!"

There was a series of audible clicks as the lock was turned into place; the door swung open and out crawled Ash. Brandr reached down to help him up, grasping his hand. When Ash stood upright, Brandr said, "Ash, your eyes… They're black."

Ash grinned menacingly and spoke in a voice that didn't belong to him, "Ash isn't here right now."

Brandr's eyes widened, but before he could do anything else he was shoved very hard by the demon-possessed boy. He hit the ground with a "Hmpf", and scrambled back to his feet, his other Guardians to his left and right. The other Asmarians started circling Ash, summoning their powers.

Kane was unsure of how to handle this. The monster was inside of his friend. How was he supposed to kill him?

Ash's head was thrown back, and laughter bellowed from his

mouth. Shadows fluttered off his body like black steam. Quinn stepped forward, tears threatening to spill over her cheeks, "Get out of him, you bastard!"

In his demonic voice, "Now, now, is that any way to speak to your future master?"

"You will never be the master of us! Asmarians will always be here to protect the world from the evil likes of you!"

Kane had to hand it to her, she could be intimidating when she wanted to be.

Aros seemed upset by her statements though. Black lightning began circling his body, starting at his ankles and wrapping up his body. Kane sensed that he was about to do something big. It appeared that others were dialed in as well. He noticed the Guardians nodding to one another and other Guild members. In unison, they lifted their hands and blasted the spot where the boy stood.

"No!" Kane and Quinn yelled at the same time, but they couldn't see what happened. The light that shone from the massive ball of energy in front of them was too bright for them to look. Kane wrapped her in a protective hug and turned away.

After a few seconds, the mages let the power go, the light subsiding. When the energy dissipated, they looked to where Ash was but discovered he no longer stood there. Someone pointed and yelled, "Look!" Ash had teleported just before the blast connected, reappearing a small distance away. He was cloaked in a thin mist of translucent darkness just staring up at the Great Tree.

Kane was immobile as others ran towards him. Ash's body turned and faced the approaching warriors. He smiled and turned back to the tree lifting a single arm and creating a fist.

Shadow and black lightning swirled around his arm, twisting from his shoulder to his fist where it began to pool. Mages began firing at him with their powers, but they were too late. With a powerful thrust, he blasted the center of the Great Tree, setting it ablaze, and then blocked their elements with his free hand.

Black veins sprouted from the tree and slowly crept around it, up and down, as flames burst from where the blast connected. The Asmarians stopped their attack and looked up, wails issued from the crowd as the tree seemed to perish. Flames erupted from its trunk and color was draining from its foliage.

Kane was distracted by the chaos and heard a gurgling sound from behind him. He whirled around to see Aros standing behind Brandr, his arm wrapped tightly around their leader's neck. Brandr was struggling to breathe.

"Let him go!" Quinn yelled, which brought the attention of the others back to the danger in front of them.

There was a smile on Ash's face, but it looked nothing like him to Kane. The boy was shorter than Brandr and Kane wondered how he was able to hold onto him. Aros stomped the back of the man's knee and let go with one hand. It became electrified. Kane noticed his hair lifting.

Brandr then suddenly twisted from his grasp, elbowing him in the face. Blood spurted from Ash's nose except it was black, rather than red. He smiled again. The static intensified. A three-foot-long blade of pure darkness protruded from his palm. Black lightning arced around it. With speed that was inhuman, he thrust the blade forward. It glided easily through the Guardian's chest.

Kane's ears were filled with screams and he didn't know if any of them belonged to him or not. Anger swelled up inside of him. He couldn't believe this was happening.

He was close enough to hear Brandr ask, "Why?"

Smiling, Ash's mouth moved, but the demon's voice answered, "Why? Because I can. And if I can, then I will." He ripped the blade back out, Brandr fell to his knees, and Ash reared back about to swing on him with a strike that would no doubt lop off the man's head.

Before it reached its destination, a tentacle of water wrapped around his wrist and yanked him back. Kane just noticed that Quinn had flanked him. He made a mental note to remind her how awesome she was after this was over. Her action gave Kane the courage to move his feet. He began his charge.

Once again, Aros disappeared and then reappeared behind his target. Only this time, his target happened to be Quinn. He snarled in her ear and she screamed. She turned to face him and his hand shot out, clasping around her throat.

Before Aros could inflict any lasting damage, the blackness of his eyes faltered, that purple hue returned and he let go of Quinn. She dove out of harm's way, looking up at him from the ground.

Ash yelled, with his very own voice, in desperation, "I've got him! He's trapped in my mind, but hurry! Kill me! That's the only way! If his vessel dies while still in the body he dies with it! Hurry, before he escapes!"

Before anyone else moved, Kane burst into the air with a lift from the wind, as if defying gravity. It was like his whole life of training depended on this moment, his focus narrowed and he knew time was of the essence. At any moment the demon could regain control and eject himself from the body or solidify his hold on Ash. He reached behind his back and grabbed two of the small throwing stars out of their pouches, one in each hand. Imbuing them with the power of the wind he hurled them simultaneously at the enemy.

One of the throwing stars embedded itself deep into Ash's stomach, and the other sliced through his neck. Blood seeped from his belly wound and spurted out of his neck, splattering the ground. As Ash fell to his knees, he made eye contact with Kane who was returning weightlessly to the ground, he smiled as if to say thanks. This was the last thing Kane wanted. Ash was the first friend he'd made in a long time. A friend that didn't judge him on his appearance or the estate in which he lived. But his home must be protected.

Ash's smile faltered. It looked like he was struggling with something and then a black cloud of smoke erupted from his body. It ejected from his back and flowed quickly down into the hole that led to the Forbidden's lair. Ash dropped to the ground.

"No!" Quinn rushed to his side, the other Guardians making their way to Brandr. They held his hand as his blood mixed with the soil.

Kane walked up to Ash, the shock hitting him. He dropped to his knees and grabbed one of his hands. A knot had worked its way into his throat. He opened his mouth to speak, but words failed him. He didn't know the right words to say if such words even existed. His vision became cloudy.

The Deity

Ash had a brief moment of reflection. Was this that whole life flashing before your eyes thing? There was always a darkness inside him, he knew that early on, but he never knew how to express it. Now he knew; it was the void of friendship, which was gone. He had met some of the greatest people he could ever hope to meet on this adventure; he smiled at Quinn as she put pressure on his neck wound, she was screaming something at him, but he couldn't hear her. It just sounded like jaded noise, like when you have earplugs in and someone tries to whisper to you.

Kane knelt beside him and looked as if he wanted to say something but even if he did Ash wouldn't have heard it. He was too busy reliving the last bit of his life when everything had changed. He wouldn't trade any of it for the world, except for maybe the whole dying part. That he could live without.

Ash only had a couple of regrets now that he was dying. He regretted never kissing Quinn or at the very least, telling her how he felt. He also regretted not dying instantly, for even in his final moments, he couldn't defeat their enemy. The walls of his vision began to narrow as he wondered what his father would think of this, but more importantly, he worried that Rick would be unable to handle it.

Quinn couldn't believe it. The brokenness she'd felt when Ash was taken didn't compare to the shattering inside her at this moment. Blood was flowing liberally from his wounds. If not for the absolute devastation she was feeling, she would probably lash out at Kane. Her anger at him for doing this bubbled just under the surface of her heartbreak. Her tears dropped from her chin and splashed the front of Ash's bloodied clothes.

"The... tree." She heard Brandr mumbling through ragged breathing. "You all... must... save... the tree."

She hadn't even thought of the tree. Quinn turned just as Leena raised her hands and conjured a massive stream of water that washed over the entirety of the Great Tree. The flames were extinguished and some of the color began to return. However, the black veins remained on its bark.

At this point, Quinn didn't think she cared if the tree died or not. She just wanted to save Ash, but she felt powerless to do so.

Brandr began to move, crawling, dragging himself toward the tree. He wasn't far away now. He reached his hand out toward the Tree. Quinn had stopped crying, either by choice or because she had no tears left. She watched the Guardian, wondering what he was about to do.

"Please. Take me. Save the boy," he told the Tree.

As the request left his lips, roots exploded from the ground and wrapped around his body. They dragged him beneath the dirt as the other Guardians exclaimed their disagreement.

Quinn could do nothing but watch, her mouth wide open.

A rush of color flooded the tree, slightly overpowering the black veins. Its leaves rustled as the branches bent and twisted toward Ash. Quinn jumped up out of the way. She felt a spark of hope ignite inside her as the branches wrapped around Ash. It lifted him off the ground and he disappeared in the foliage. The bundle of sticks and leaves began to shine with a bright golden light.

After a minute Quinn began wondering if something was wrong. Did the Tree have enough power to bring him back? She had to believe it could.

Where am I?

Ash awoke in a place he'd never been before. Everything was pure white. It was almost blinding. The only color in this void was that of his own body. He stood up, feeling weightless.

"Hello?" he said to no one in particular.

In the distance, a small dot appeared and then it took shape as it got close. He could tell that it was humanoid. He wasn't sure if he should prepare for a fight or not but thought it best to be ready for anything. He clenched his fists as the thing's details became more clear.

It was a woman, sort of. She resembled the fairies that he'd seen during his first night in Asmaria. The creature was only a foot tall, but her light brown hair was the length of her body. Her skin was but a shade darker than her hair. She wore a crown of twigs and flowers around her head. Ash could see her eyes; they shone brightly with hues of blue, pink, and green all swirling together.

Her emerald dress flowed through the air. She had wings that resembled those of a butterfly but were more translucent. Ash was stricken with curiosity as to who or what she was.

"Hello, Ash." Her voice sounded as if it were a conglomerate of a thousand other voices. He didn't know if he should be scared or not. He could feel the immense power radiating from her as she spoke.

"Are you a fairy?" he asked.

"I've been called many things. You know me as the Great Tree. However, in this form, you can call me Gethin. No, I'm not a fairy. Your mind would be shattered if I told you of my true identity, for the weight is too much to bear. I can take whichever shape I choose while in your head."

Ash didn't want his mind to shatter. "Gethin," he repeated. "So, where am I? I'm dead right?"

"For now."

"What do you mean?"

"I have the power to bring you back, but it all depends on you."

Ash was confused. How could it depend on him if she was the one with the power? She answered his question as if reading his thoughts.

"You have to choose life. If your will isn't strong enough, then my power can't save you. Do you have the will to live, Ash?"

He thought about it for a moment, "I do. I failed my friends. I couldn't forgive myself if I just died without taking that demon with me."

Gethin chuckled, "I knew you'd make the right choice. But you must promise me something."

"What is it?"

Her voice became more serious, "You must save me as well."

The entity moved closer, merely inches away now. She revealed a small green light in the center of her chest, just under her neck. It was dim and pulsating.

"This is my life force. The demon, Aros, has poisoned me. My current tree form will die, there is no stopping that. I will share knowledge with all the Asmarians with the information that shall save me, and thus save all of you. Be warned, your enemy has only just begun. His power will increase so you must be ready. Now, you must go, already I am becoming weak."

She moved forward and reached out as if to touch Ash, but he said, "Wait. I have so many questions."

Gethin smiled sadly, "I know you do."

With that, she touched him on the forehead and his vision went black.

Sound was the first to return. He could hear someone crying. It sounded like Quinn. Why was she so sad? Next, he could feel the ground beneath him. It was hard. His eyes slowly parted and the sun was blinding. When his vision adjusted he looked down to see Quinn's head on his chest. Her body was heaving with sobs. He noticed that his shirt was soaked in blood.

Kane sat next to him with tears in his eyes but he remained silent, cradling Ash's head. The recent events came back to him in a rush. He looked at Kane, smiled, and said, "You tried to kill me."

Kane laughed, "Yeah, luckily I was unsuccessful."

Ash moved to sit up and his two friends helped him upright. He patted his body, checking for wounds. The holes in his neck and stomach had been mended and there was no pain, just a slight grogginess, like he'd taken a long nap. Ash looked around him.

The Guardians and other Guild members looked rough. Many of them were sobbing loudly. Something felt off and it took a moment for him to notice what it was. Brandr was missing.

"What happened?" he asked them.

Quinn was still choked up but Kane answered, "Brandr asked the Tree to take him and save you. His sacrifice gave the boost needed to bring you back."

Shortly after Ash was revived, the Guardians ordered anyone who was able to search the pit beneath them to try apprehending the Forbidden. After scouring the entirety of the pit it was clear that they had fled immediately. It was as if they were never there.

Ash couldn't believe it. He wasn't sure if he'd ever forgive himself for this. However, he knew that now wasn't the time to dwell on it. He got up and walked over to the Guardians.

"I need to talk to the Guild. All of them."

Kane sat in the audience next to Quinn as Ash shared with all of the Guild what happened in his head. Now and then he would hear a snicker at something Ash said. Looking around, he noticed that many of the mages were shaking their heads in disbelief.

He couldn't believe it himself, but being friends with Ash, Kane knew that he wouldn't just make this stuff up. The Great Tree was a mystery to most Asmarians, who knew what kind of things the Tree could conjure up?

Once finished, Ash sat down and there was a brief moment of silence and then someone in the crowd yelled, "How do we know we can trust him? Aros was inside of him!"

The outburst caught like a wildfire, spreading through the mages, many of them calling for Ash's imprisonment. They became restless and began jumping down to the stage area where Ash sat unperturbed. Kane wouldn't fail him again.

Hurling himself through the air, Kane landed softly in front of Ash, pulling two small blades from their sheaths. He stood in a fighting stance, prepared to fight off his comrades to save his friend. The Guardians were trying to gain control but the crowd was simply too many.

Bora stepped in front of Kane, a fierce look on her face. She began swinging her arms as if throwing punches, but instead, it was the wind that blasted the mob back. Avani jumped next to her and raised his hands. His arms trembled as the ground swallowed the Guild members up to their necks. He held them there until the grumbling ceased and then addressed the crowd.

"No one will harm a hair on this boy's head. Is that clear?"

A resounding 'yes' answered him. Relief swept through Kane as the mages were all released and the ground returned to its original state.

It had been a week since Ash died and was brought back to life by the Great Tree. People often looked at him with disdain as he passed by, but it didn't bother him as much as he thought they hoped for.

He often visited the Tree but it had yet to divulge any information. Already were the black veins of poison spreading across its trunk. Ash had become virtually inseparable from Quinn. They spent every possible moment together. He still hadn't told her of his true feelings for her. There were more important things to worry about.

It was a full moon and the two of them walked down the street. Flames burned in the torches lining the streets, casting a soft orange glow in front of them. The fountain of the first Guardian came into view and sitting there was Kane.

They greeted each other and then Ash began to feel a buzz in the pit of his stomach, something pulling him toward the center of the island. By the looks on their faces, he assumed his friends felt it too. Ash took off for the Great Tree.

His friends were hot on his heels as they sprinted through the jungle. The Tree was pulsating and when they arrived at its base, he noticed they were not the first to arrive. He waited impatiently, pacing back and forth. Nothing was happening. Were they supposed to do something? More and more Asmarians poured in around the Tree, waiting for it to tell them what to do.

Finally, the branches of the Tree bent down. Ash saw them wrapping around the others' heads and then their eyes getting wide. The same happened to him. As the branch made contact he heard the voice in his head. It was the same legion of voices he'd heard while dead.

There are those in your midst who aim to gain power by tearing comrades down. Be wary of them. To save our world you must send three warriors to the kingdom once lost at sea. Buried in sand you shall find the key to my survival. But be warned, the shadows rise with more power than before.

The riddle ended and the branches released the Asmarians. Ash looked around and everyone seemed to have the same look on their face. He assumed they all heard the same message but to be sure, he asked his friends what the message said. They repeated exactly what he'd heard in his head.

"Three champions," Quinn said, "a kingdom lost at sea, and the key to the Great Tree's survival. What does any of that mean? What's with the riddles?"

New Flames

Ash sat in the audience at the Guild building with Kane and Quinn. Ballots were being collected, although they weren't required to vote for the new Guardian. He still felt guilty about Brandr sacrificing himself to save him. Even if he did know any of the names on the ballot, he wasn't sure that he'd want to pick a new fire Guardian.

He watched as the Guardians rifled through the ballots, tallying up the votes. They picked four names of their strongest mages but left the decision up to the people.

Avani turned, there was a look on his face that Ash couldn't quite read. He'd been nicer to Ash recently, but the look reminded him of how he looked when he'd met the grumpy Guardian.

"Ember Broderick," he yelled out, "please join us."

A man rose a few rows away from Ash; he turned and made eye contact with him. The look gave Ash an uneasy feeling. The man climbed down the steps and joined the other Guardians.

Avani put an orange wreath on his shoulders and congratulated him on being selected as the new Guardian. Ember stared at Ash the whole time, even while giving his acceptance speech.

"It's an honor and a privilege to be selected as your new Guardian of the flame. It's reassuring to know that there are enough like-minded warriors among us to bring about an era of prosperity to our people. It will be my pleasure to serve you all."

"Thank you, Ember." Leena called out, "And with that, I'd like to introduce you all to the new lead Guardian, Bora."

Bore stepped up, "The circumstances that bring about a new Guardian is almost always tragic. I accept this position with much sadness in my heart. However, I vow to fill Brandr's shoes as the lead Guardian to the best of my ability."

The Guild was dismissed and everyone dispersed from the building. Rick was at home waiting for Ash to return. The man was allowed to stay in Asmaria but was given strict guidelines as to where he could go. He wasn't allowed to attend any meetings of importance and could only move about with an escort. Ash wasn't ready to go back home to him yet.

He and Quinn said goodbye to Kane and he convinced her to go for a walk. They wandered down to the small pond on the outskirts of the city.

Frogs with yellow spots hopped into the water as the two disturbed their sunbaths. There was a bench carved into a large stone at the edge of the water. They sat down and Ash took his shoes off, and dipped his toes into the cool pond.

"So I've been thinking." He told her.

She jabbed, "I've warned you about that."

They giggled and he nudged her with his elbow. "Who do you think the Guardians will send to find the key to saving the Tree?"

"There will be time to worry about that later." She said, laying her head on his shoulder.

He took her hand in his, wondering if she would pull away. When she didn't, he gripped it tighter and laid his head on top of hers. They sat in the same position for a long time. Ash didn't know how much time had passed, lost in the elation he felt. He was happy.

Acknowledgments

First of all, I must give all glory to God. Without Him, I would not have the mind to create a book.

I also want to thank you, the reader. Thank you so much for reading my book! If you enjoyed reading through this adventure please leave a review. Reviews are essential for us indie authors to continue doing the work we love!

Next, thank you to my family for the continued support and for dealing with my constant typing away at the keys. I couldn't do it without you.

Remember, if you've ever considered writing, just get to it! Start today, chase your dreams, and keep bringing words to life.

About The Author

DC Sumner is a native of Arkansas where he graduated high school and college with a BA in Criminology. He also has a wife and two daughters, aged 4 and 14. DC is also a staff sergeant in the U.S. Air Force as a Unit Training Manager.

Mr. Sumner found his love for reading in high school where he read books such as Percy Jackson and the Lightning Thief series, The Hunger Games, and Harry Potter. He has wanted to write a book for many years and began his writing journey in April of 2023 with this book.

DC Sumner is also a major fan of TV shows such as The Office, Parks and Recreation, and Brooklyn 99. If you would like to know more about DC, you can find him on TikTok, Facebook, and Instagram or go to his website: DCSumner.com.

www.ingramcontent.com/pod-product-compliance
Lightning Source LLC
Chambersburg PA
CBHW060455300726
48975CB00008B/2520